You know you want to read
ALL the Pizza and Taco books!

WHO'S THE BEST?

BEST PARTY EVER!

SUPER-AWESOME COMIC!

TOO COOL FOR SCHOOL!
(Coming in Summer 2022)

SUPER-AWESOME COMIC!

STEPHEN SHASKAN

A STEPPING STONE BOOK™

Random House 🏠 New York

To my super-awesome agent,
Teresa Kietlinski

Copyright © 2021 by Stephen Shaskan
All rights reserved. Published in the United States by Random House Children's Books,
a division of Penguin Random House LLC, New York.
Random House and the colophon are registered trademarks and RH Graphic with
the book design is a trademark of Penguin Random House LLC.
Visit us on the Web! rhcbooks.com
Educators and librarians, for a variety of teaching tools, visit us at RHTeachersLibrarians.com

Library of Congress Cataloging-in-Publication Data
Names: Shaskan, Stephen, author, illustrator.
Title: Pizza and Taco : super-awesome comic! / Stephen Shaskan.
Description: First edition. | New York : Random House Children's Books, [2021] | Audience:
Ages 5–8 | Audience: Grades 2–3 | Summary: Best friends Pizza and Taco put their drawing
skills and wild imaginations to good use by writing a comic book together.
Identifiers: LCCN 2020046320 | ISBN 978-0-593-37603-4 (hardcover) |
ISBN 978-0-593-37604-1 (library binding) | ISBN 978-0-593-37605-8 (ebook)
Subjects: LCSH: Graphic novels. | CYAC: Graphic novels. | Best friends—Fiction. |
Friendship—Fiction. | Pizza—Fiction. | Tacos—Fiction. | Comic books, strips, etc.—Fiction.
Classification: LCC PZ7.7.S4548 Piv 2021 | DDC 741.5/973—dc23

MANUFACTURED IN CHINA
10 9 8 7 6 5 4 3 2 1
First Edition
Random House Children's Books supports the First Amendment and celebrates the right to read.

Contents

Chapter 1

Pizza and Taco Have an Idea

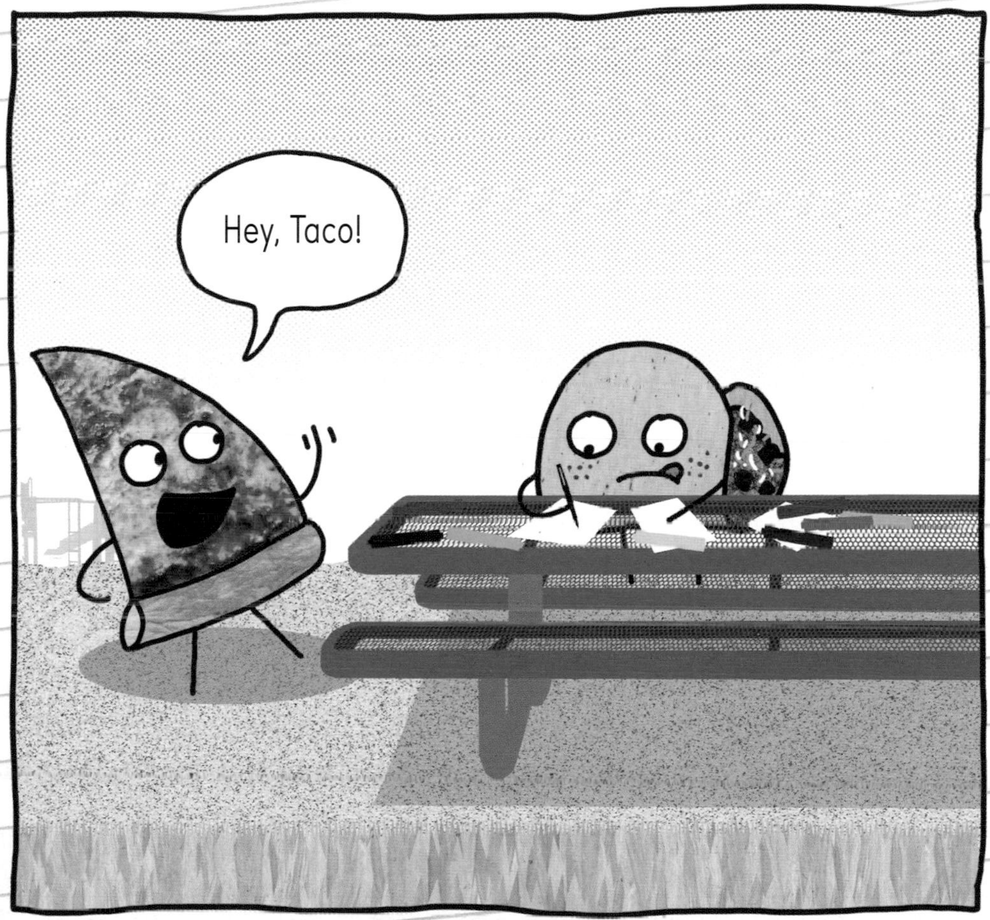
Hey, Taco!

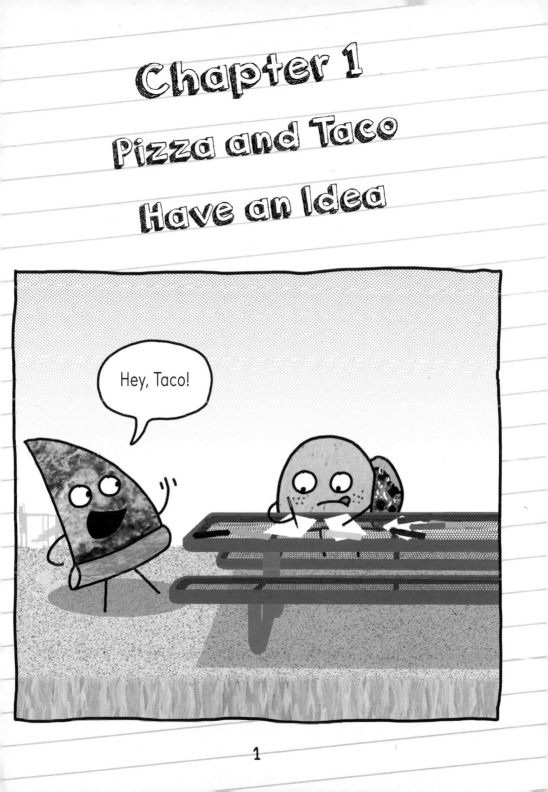

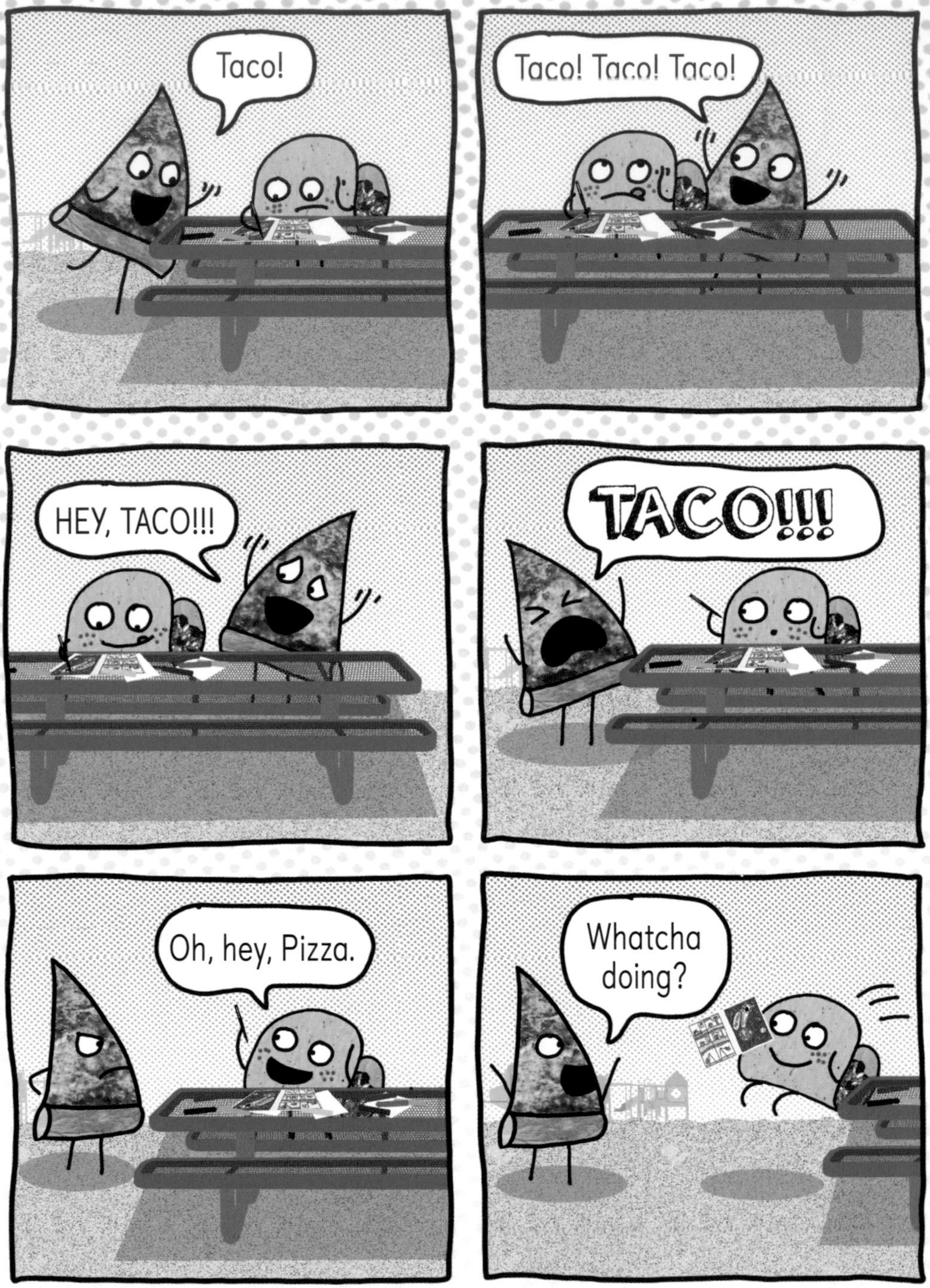
Taco!
Taco! Taco! Taco!
HEY, TACO!!!
TACO!!!
Oh, hey, Pizza.
Whatcha doing?

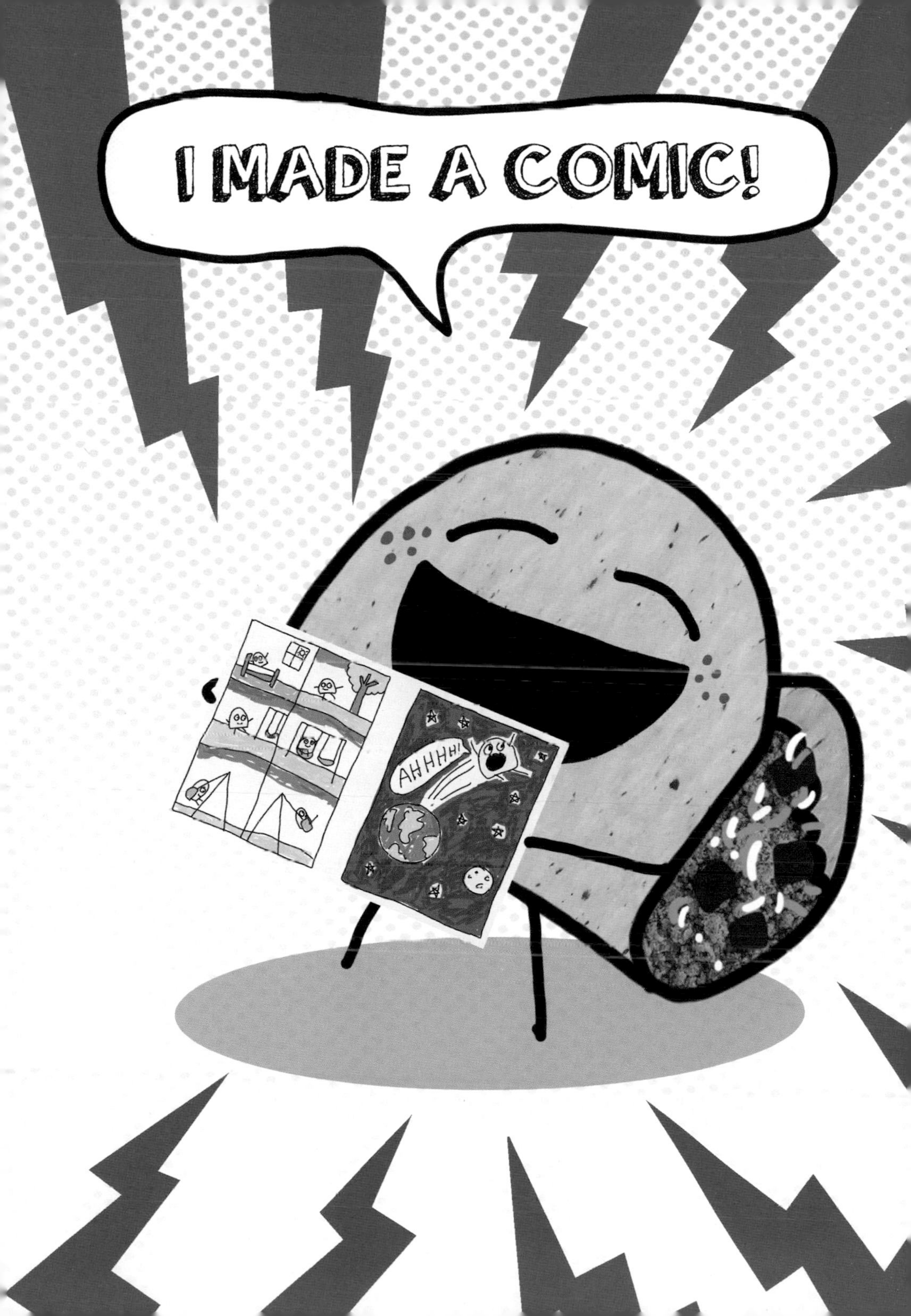
I MADE A COMIC!
AHHHH!

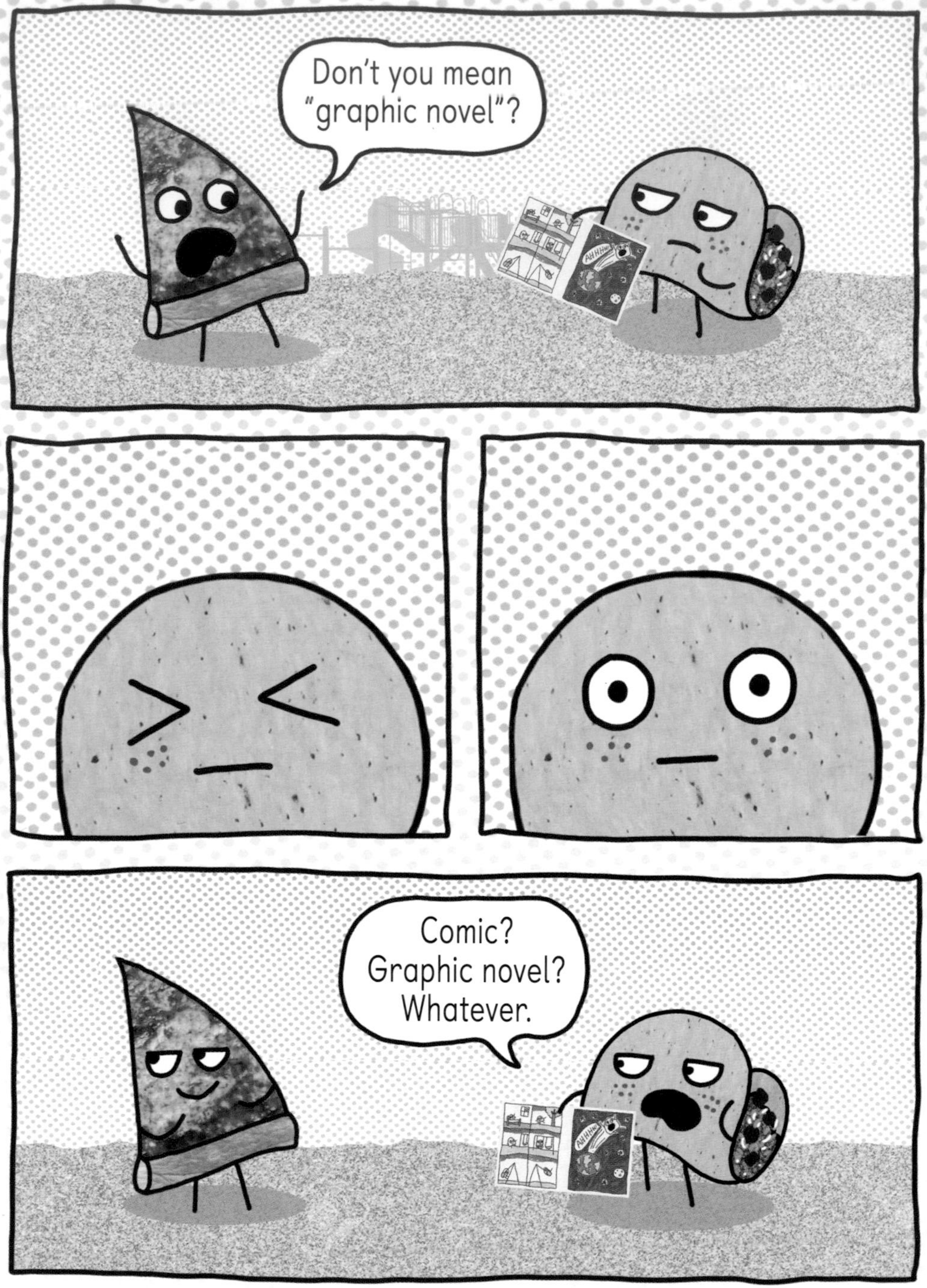
Don’t you mean “graphic novel”?
Comic? Graphic novel? Whatever.

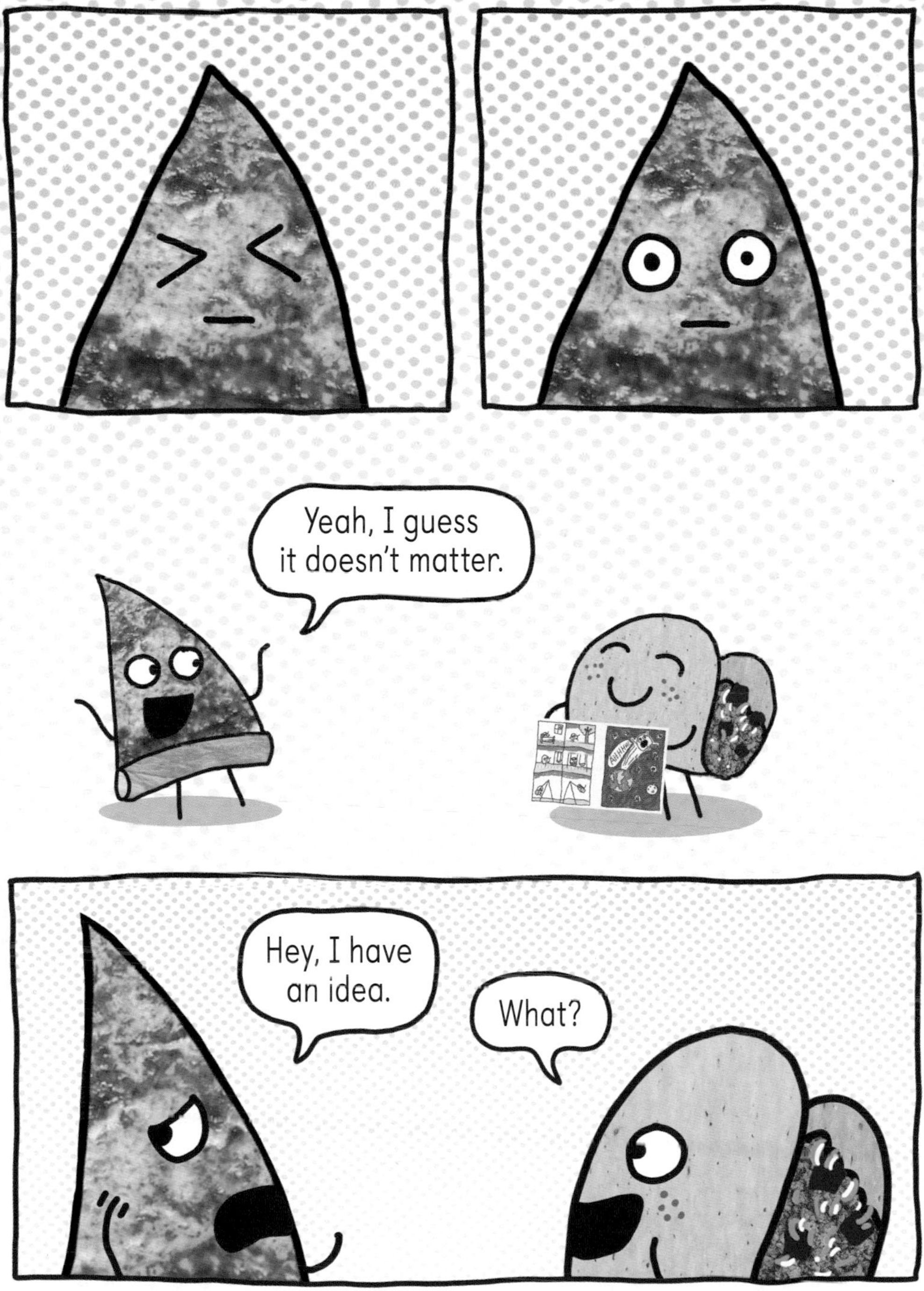
Yeah, I guess
it doesn't matter.
Hey, I have
an idea.
What?

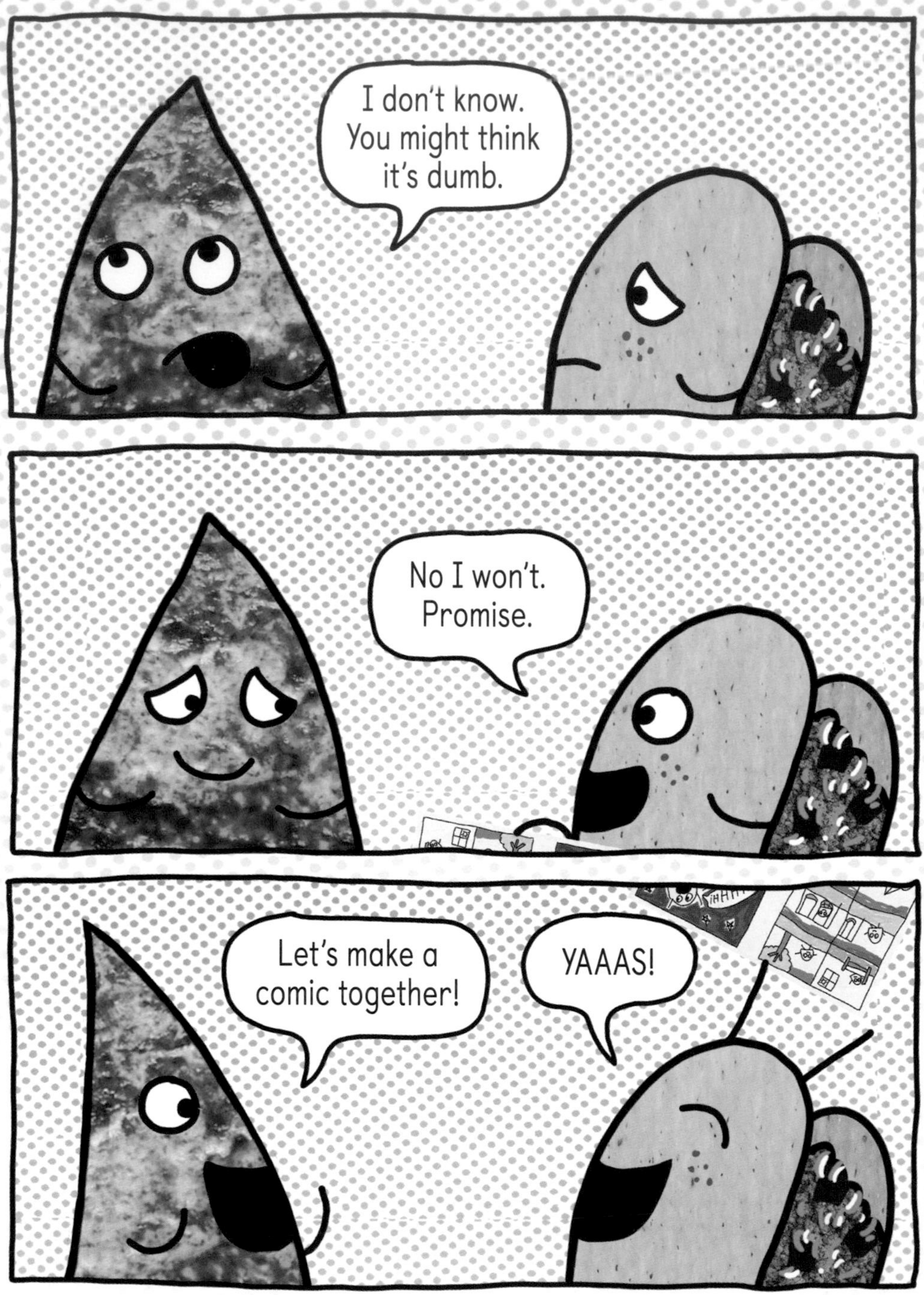
I don't know. You might think it's dumb.
No I won't. Promise.
Let's make a comic together!
YAAAS!

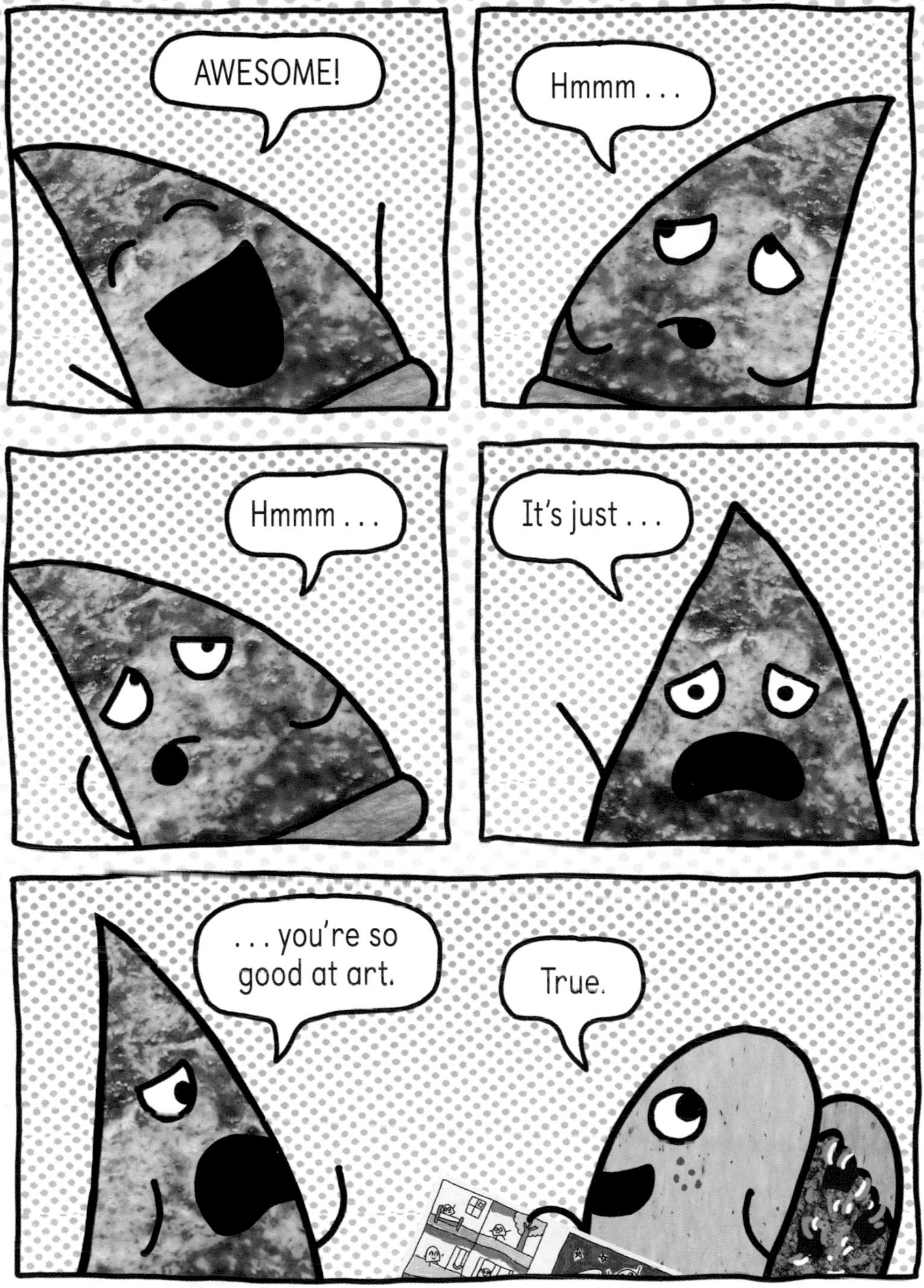
AWESOME!
Hmmm . . .
Hmmm . . .
It's just . . .
. . . you're so good at art.
True.

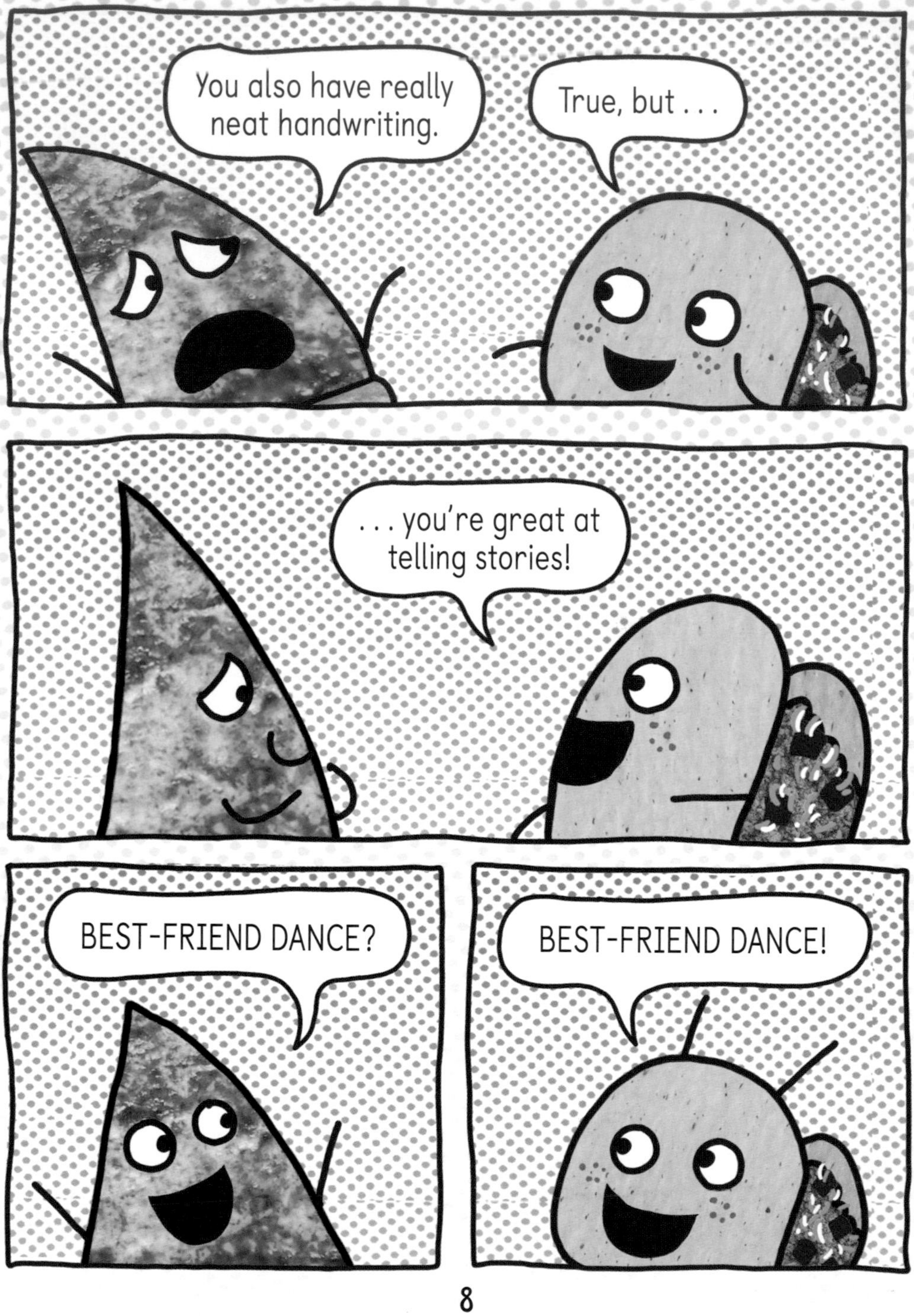
You also have really neat handwriting.
True, but . . .
. . . you're great at telling stories!
BEST-FRIEND DANCE?
BEST-FRIEND DANCE!

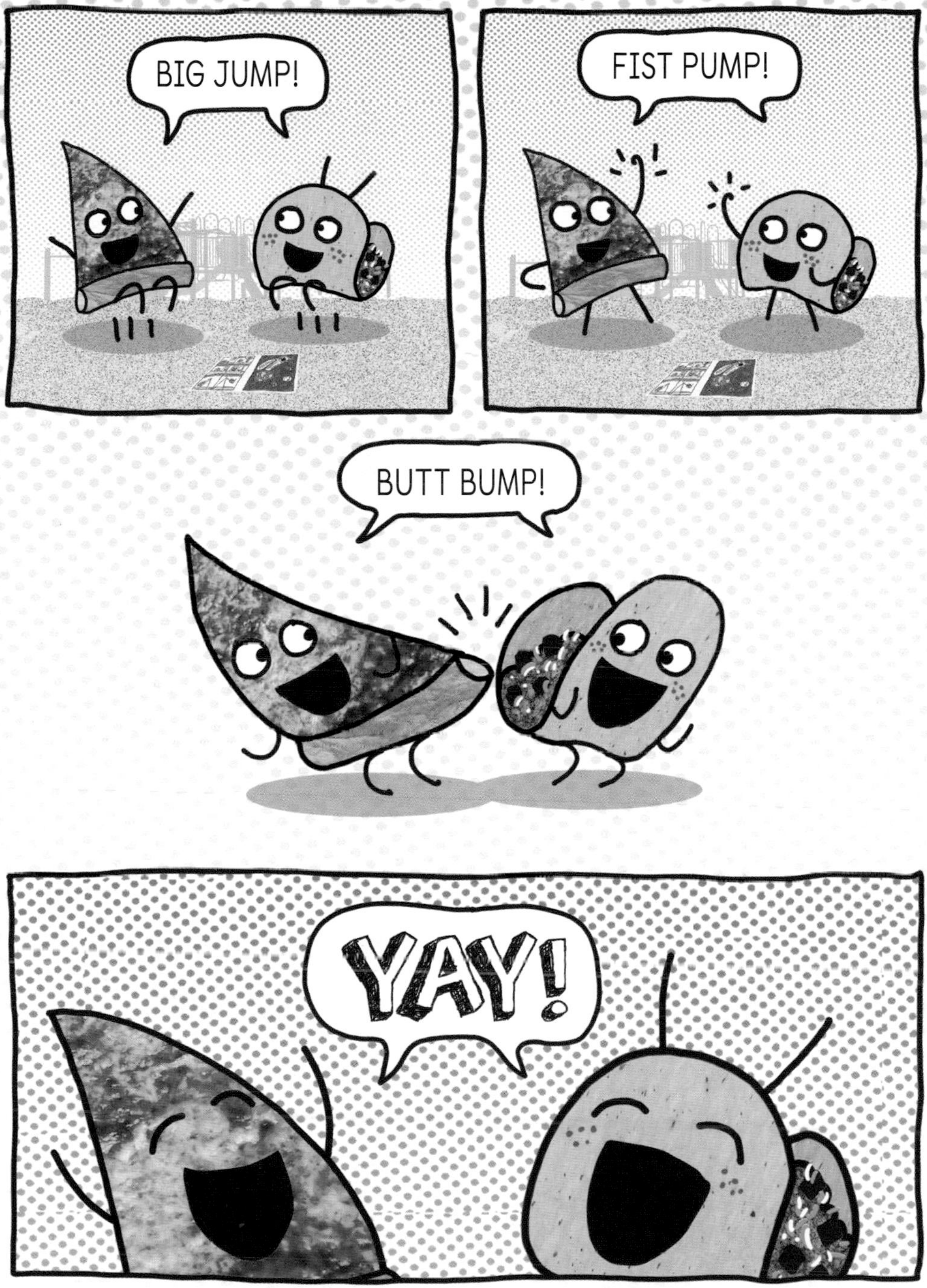
BIG JUMP!
FIST PUMP!
BUTT BUMP!
YAY!

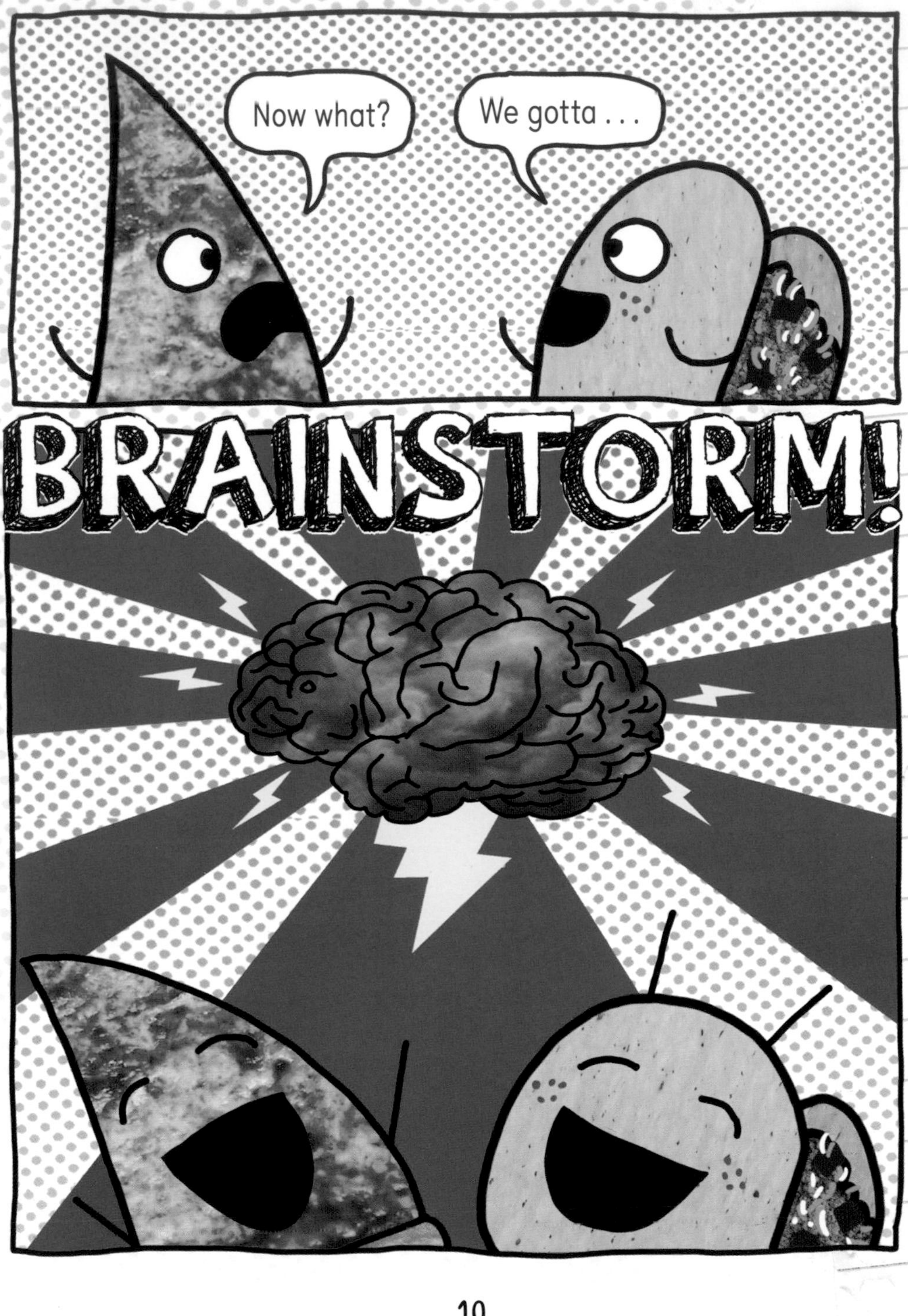
Now what?
We gotta . . .
BRAINSTORM!

Chapter 2
Pizza and Taco Brainstorm!

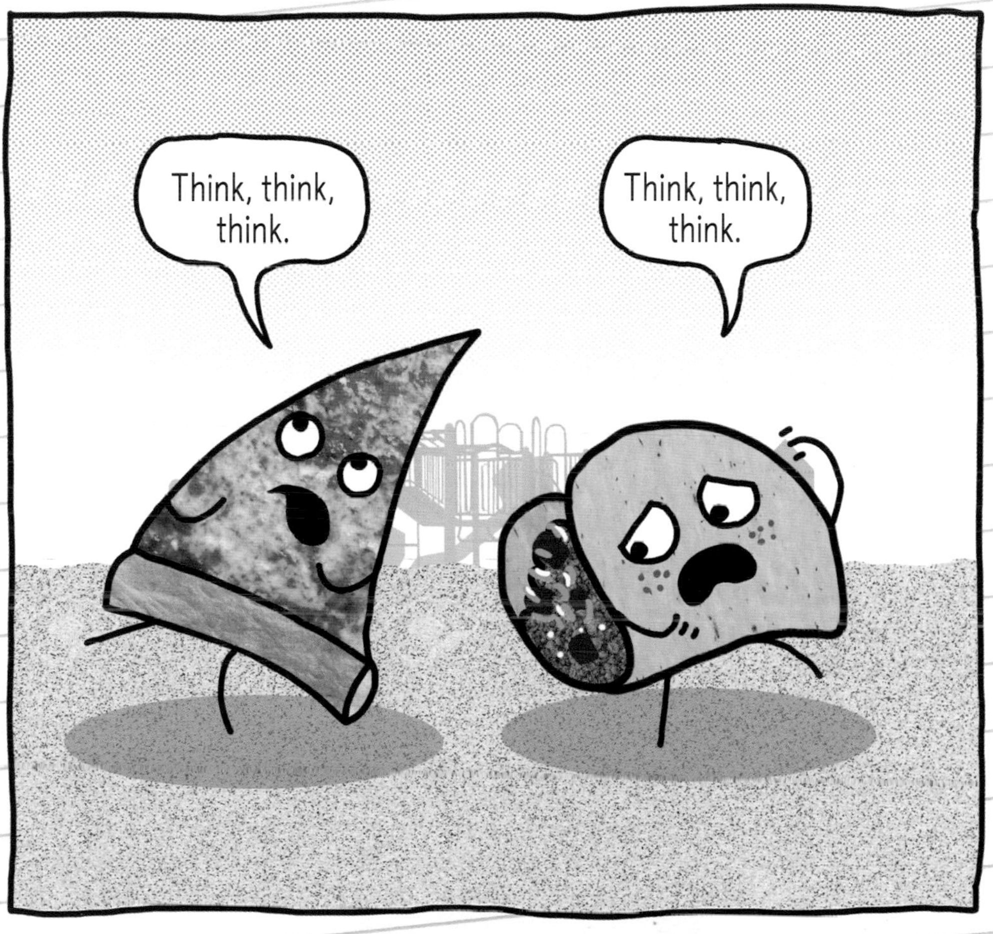
Think, think, think.
Think, think, think.

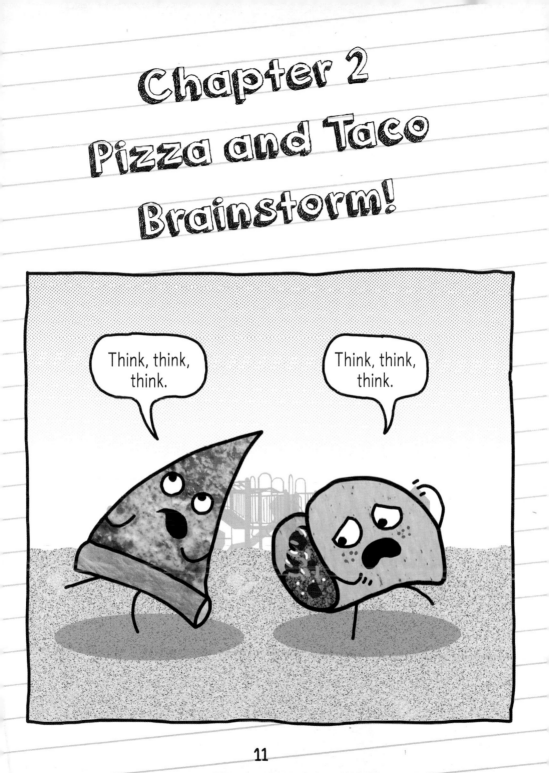

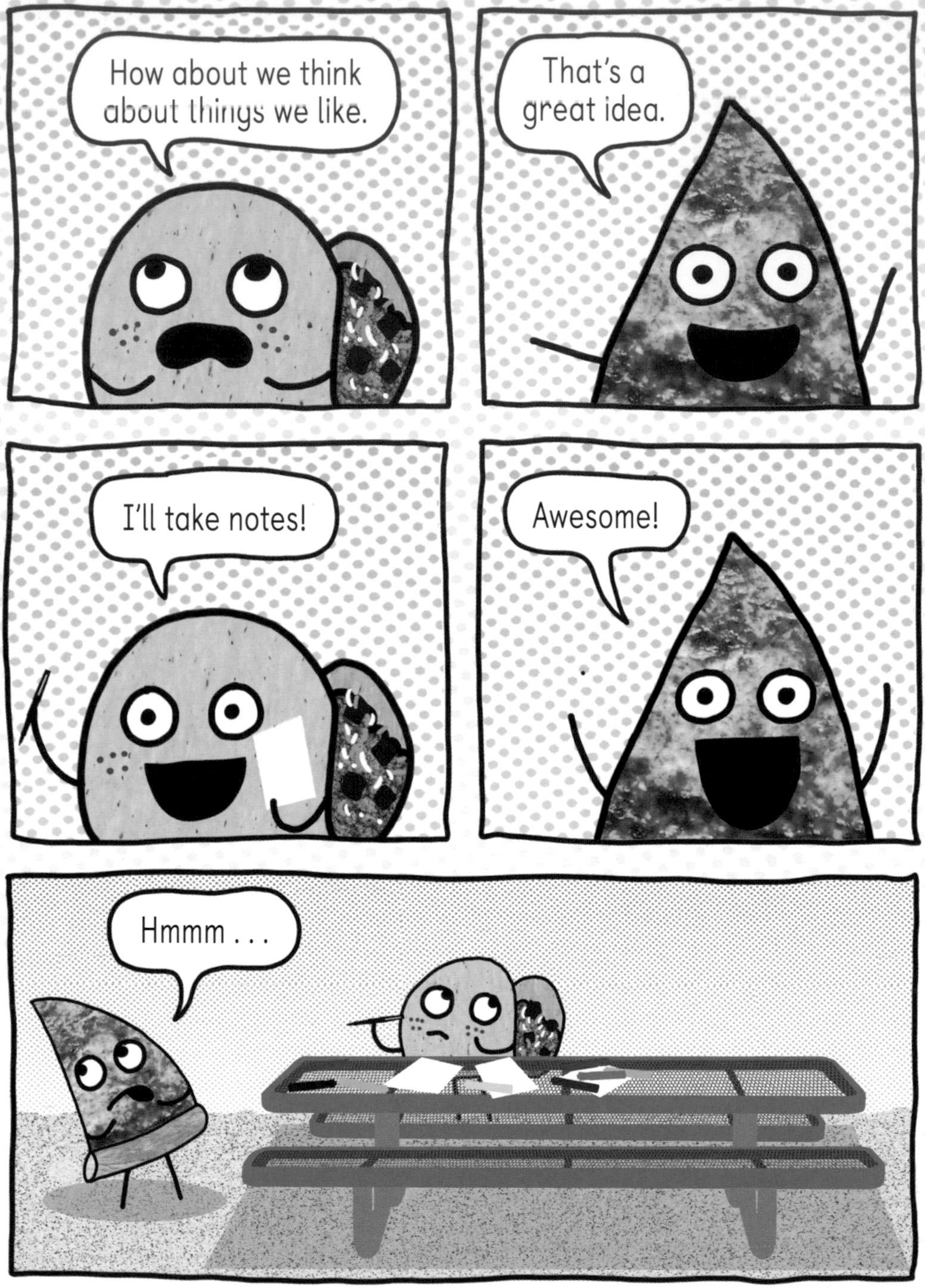
How about we think about things we like.
That's a great idea.
I'll take notes!
Awesome!
Hmmm . . .

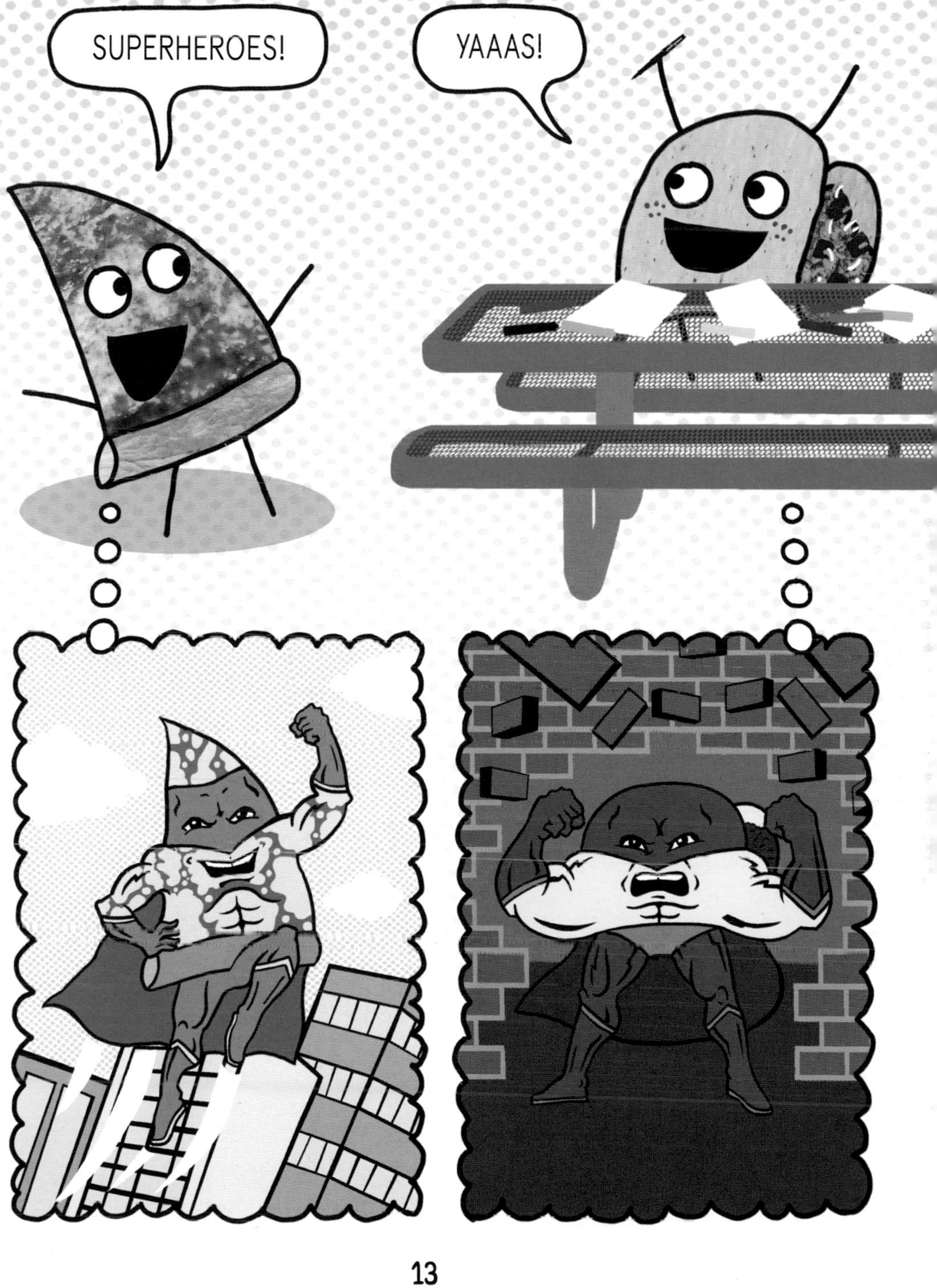
SUPERHEROES!
YAAAS!

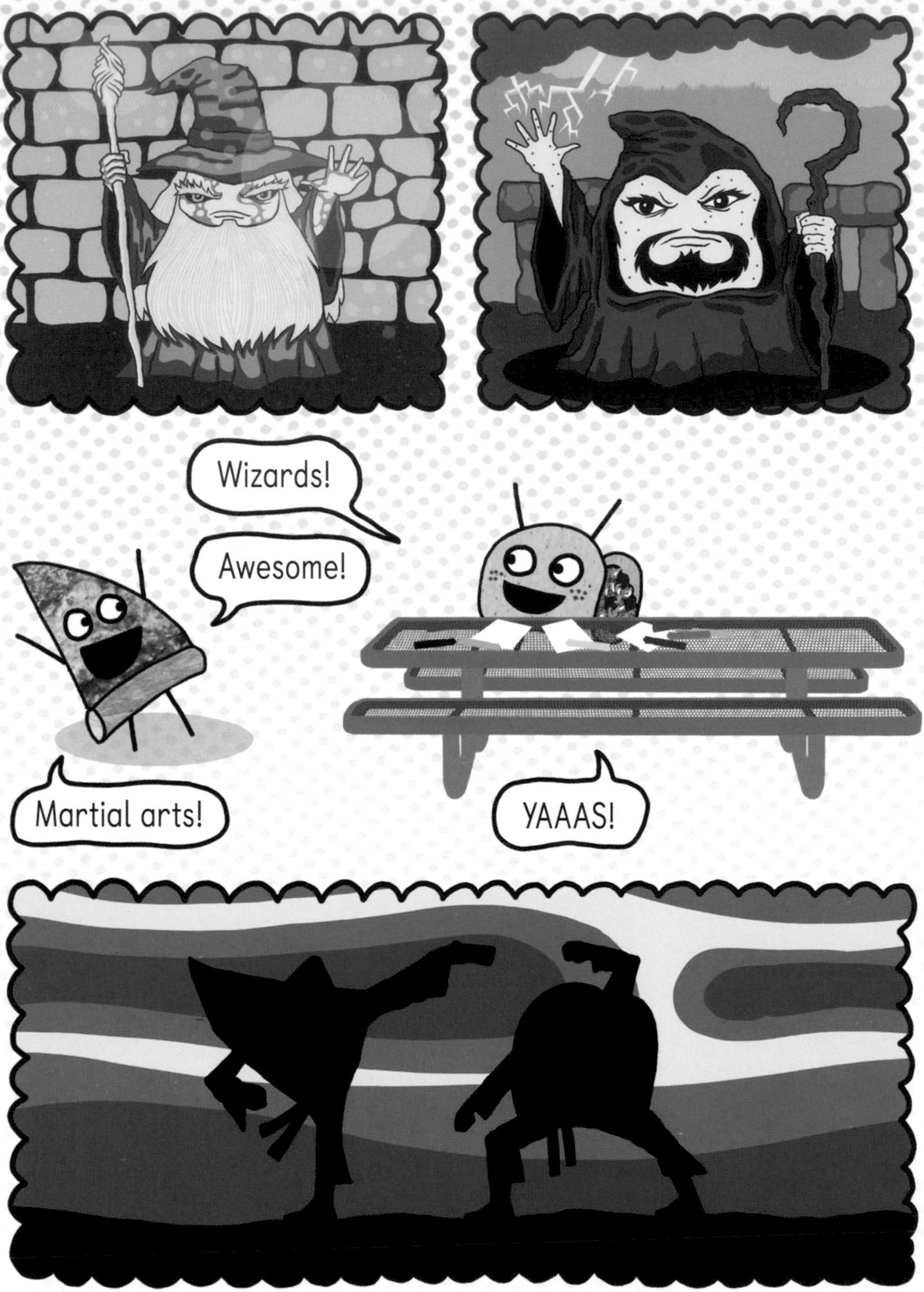
Wizards!
Awesome!
Martial arts!
YAAAS!

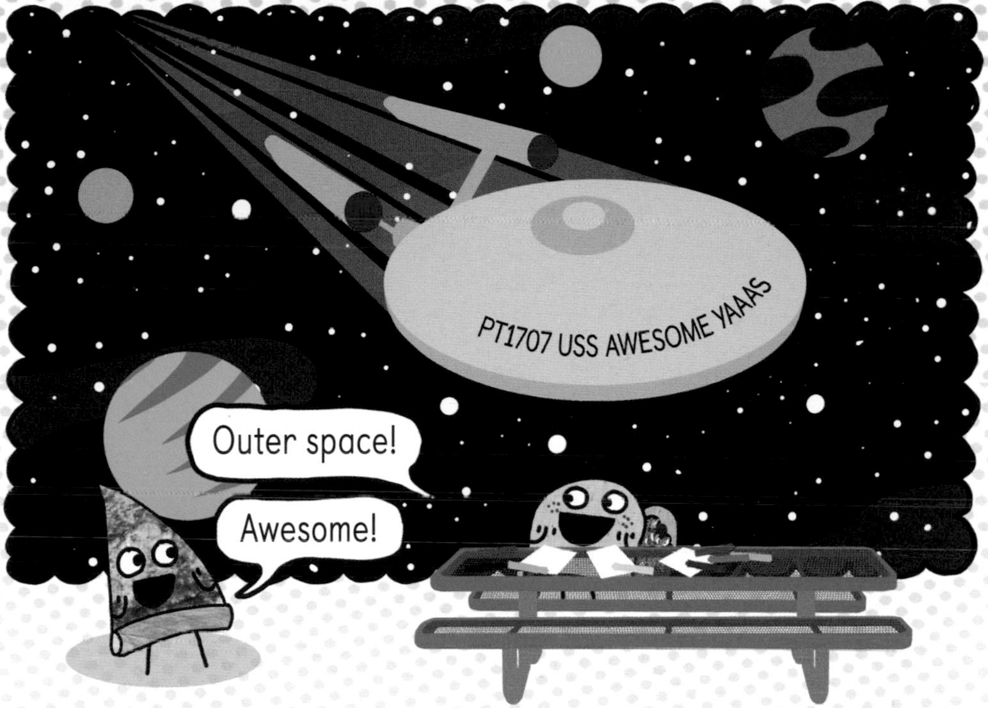
PT1707 USS AWESOME YAAAS
Outer space!
Awesome!
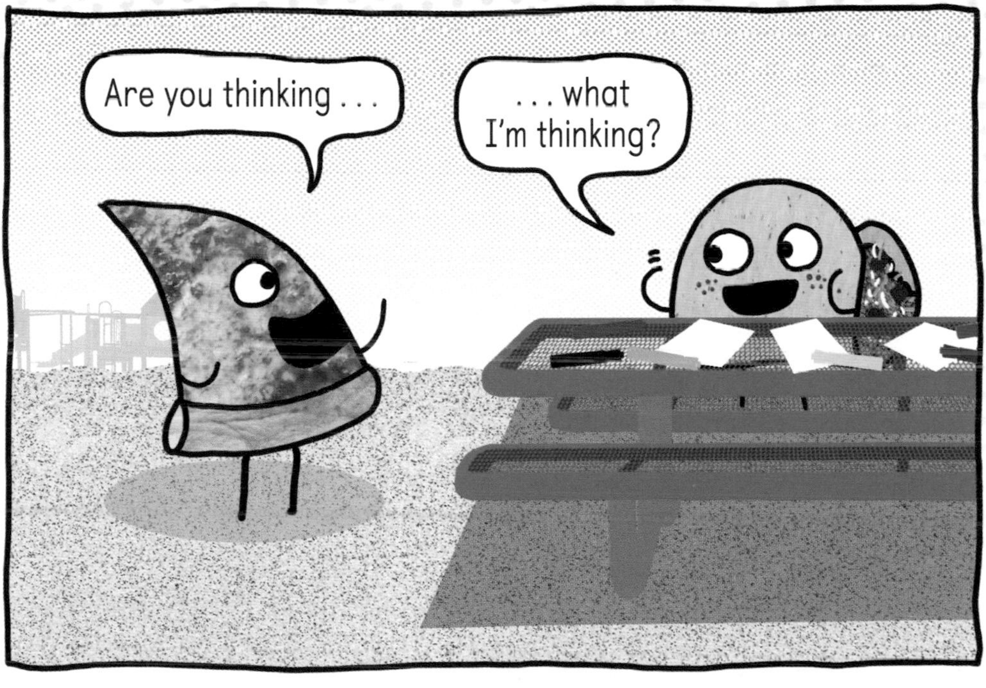
Are you thinking . . .
. . . what I'm thinking?

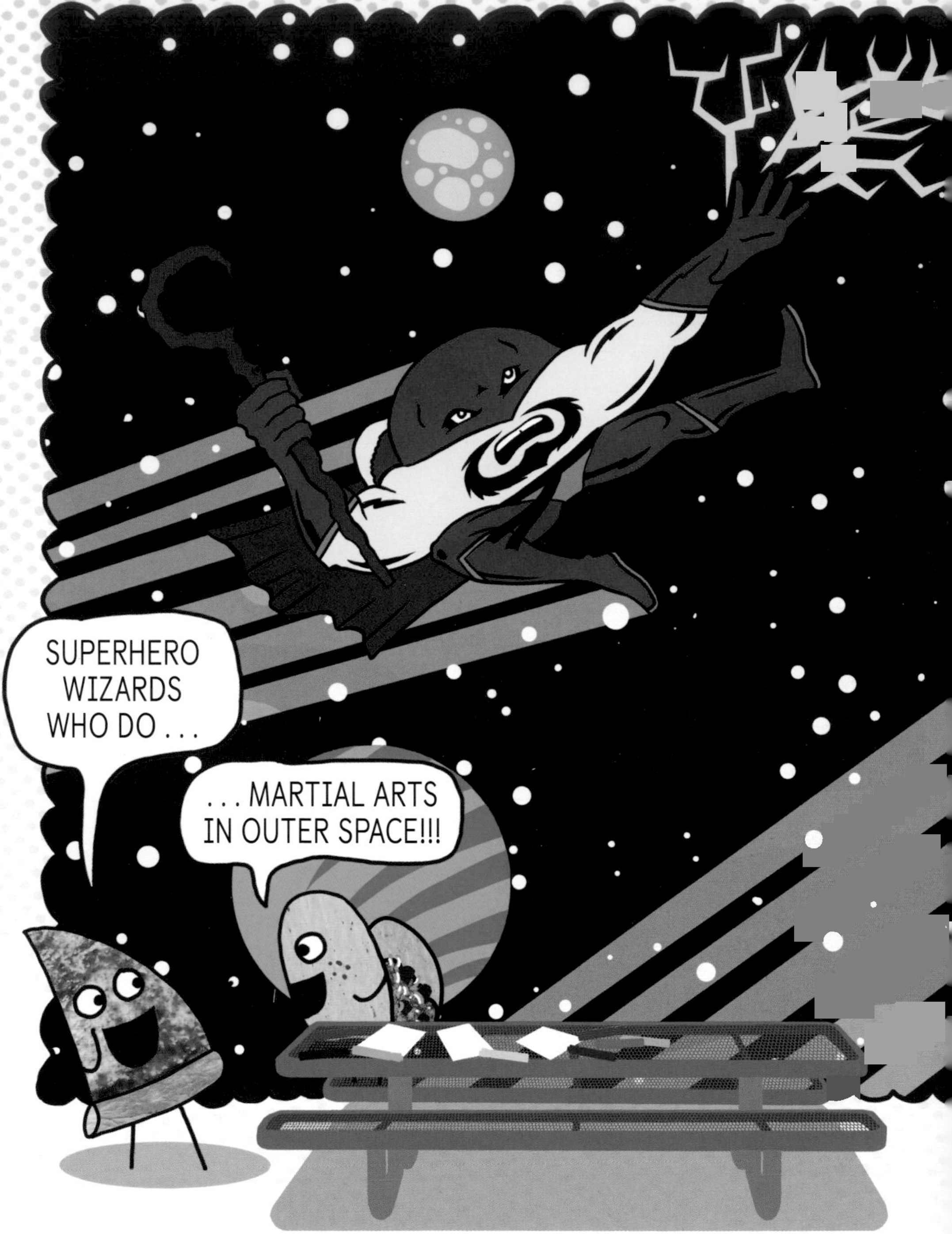
SUPERHERO WIZARDS WHO DO . . .
. . . MARTIAL ARTS IN OUTER SPACE!!!

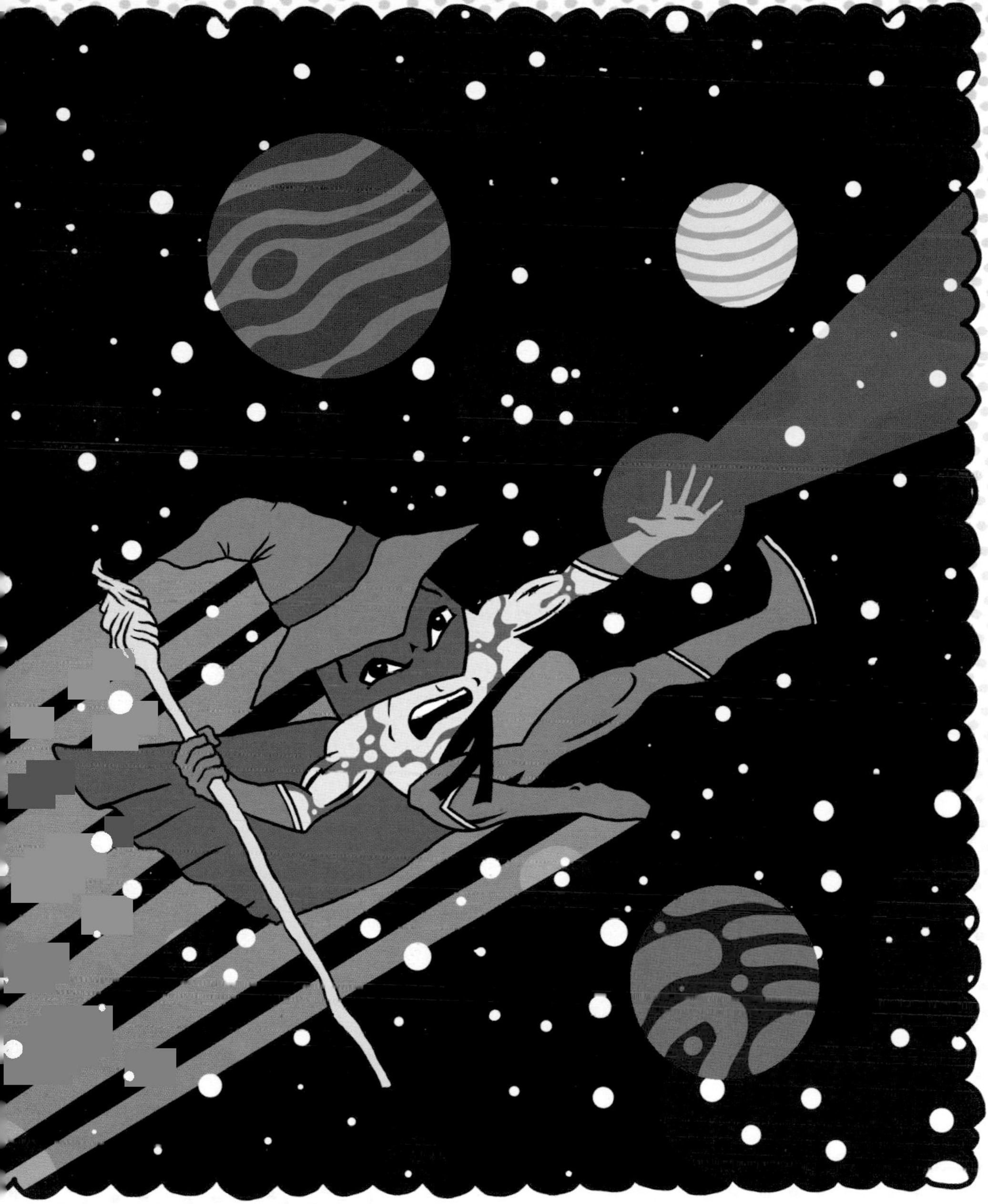

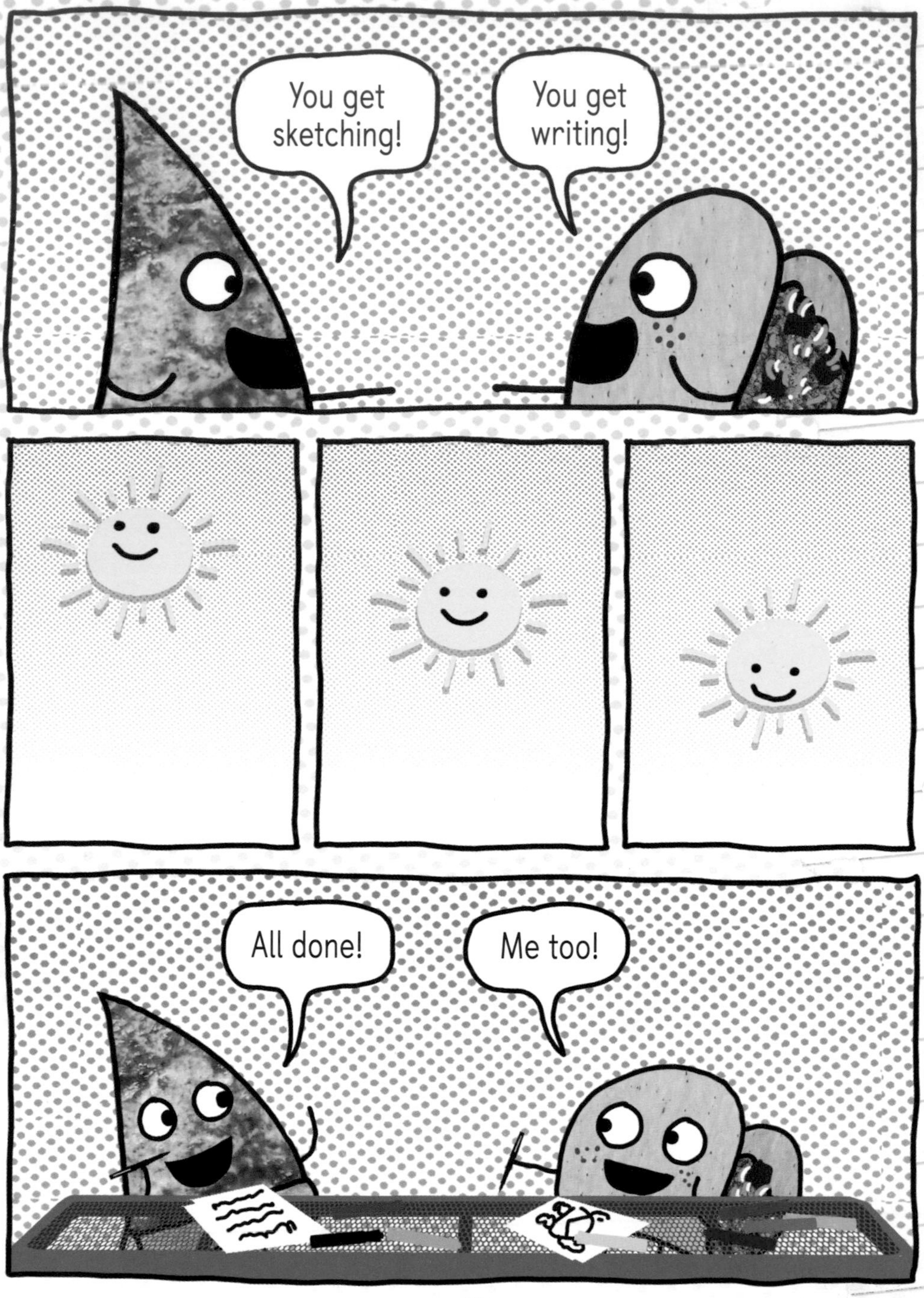
You get sketching!
You get writing!
All done!
Me too!

Chapter 3

Pizza and Taco Create Character Sketches

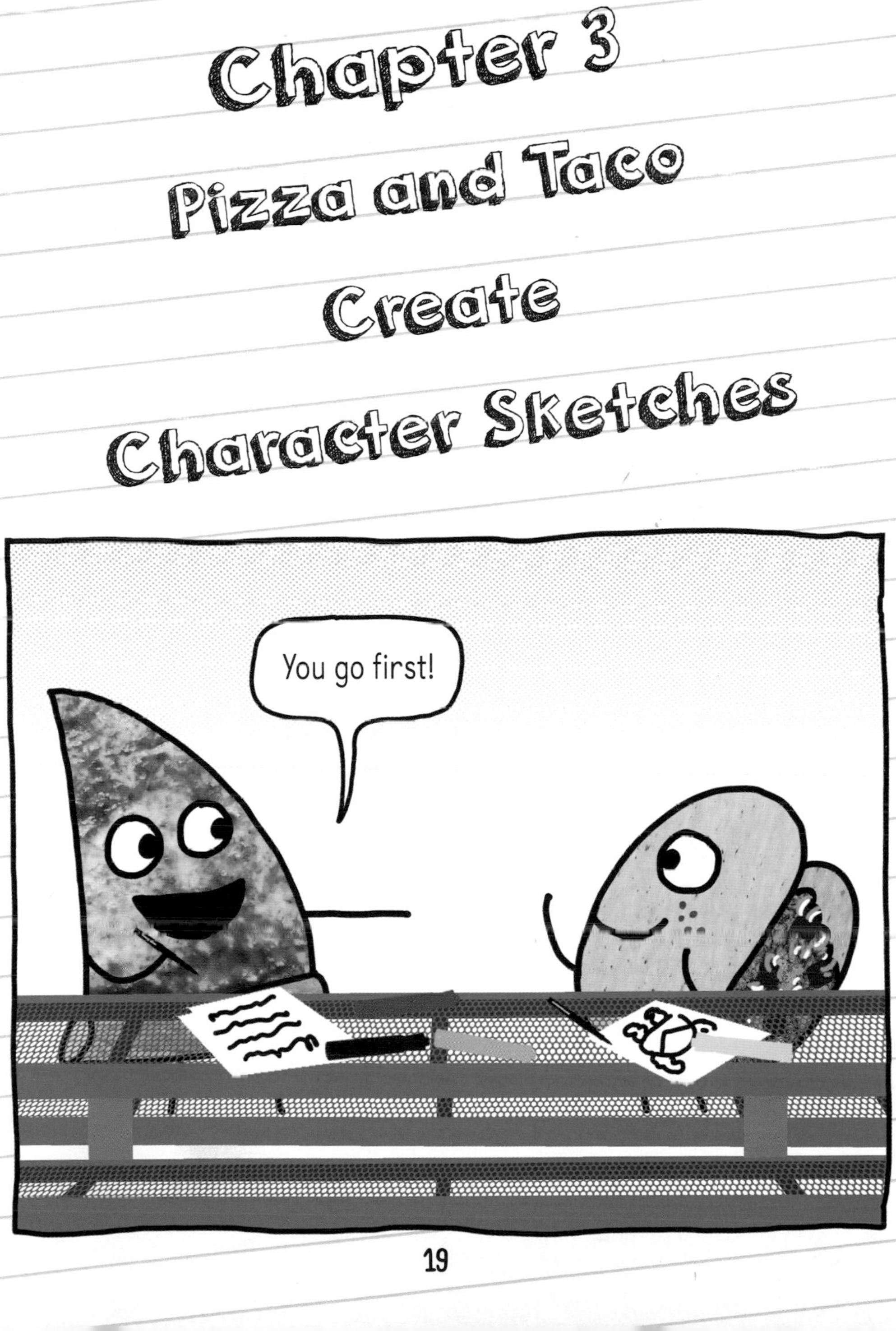

You go first!

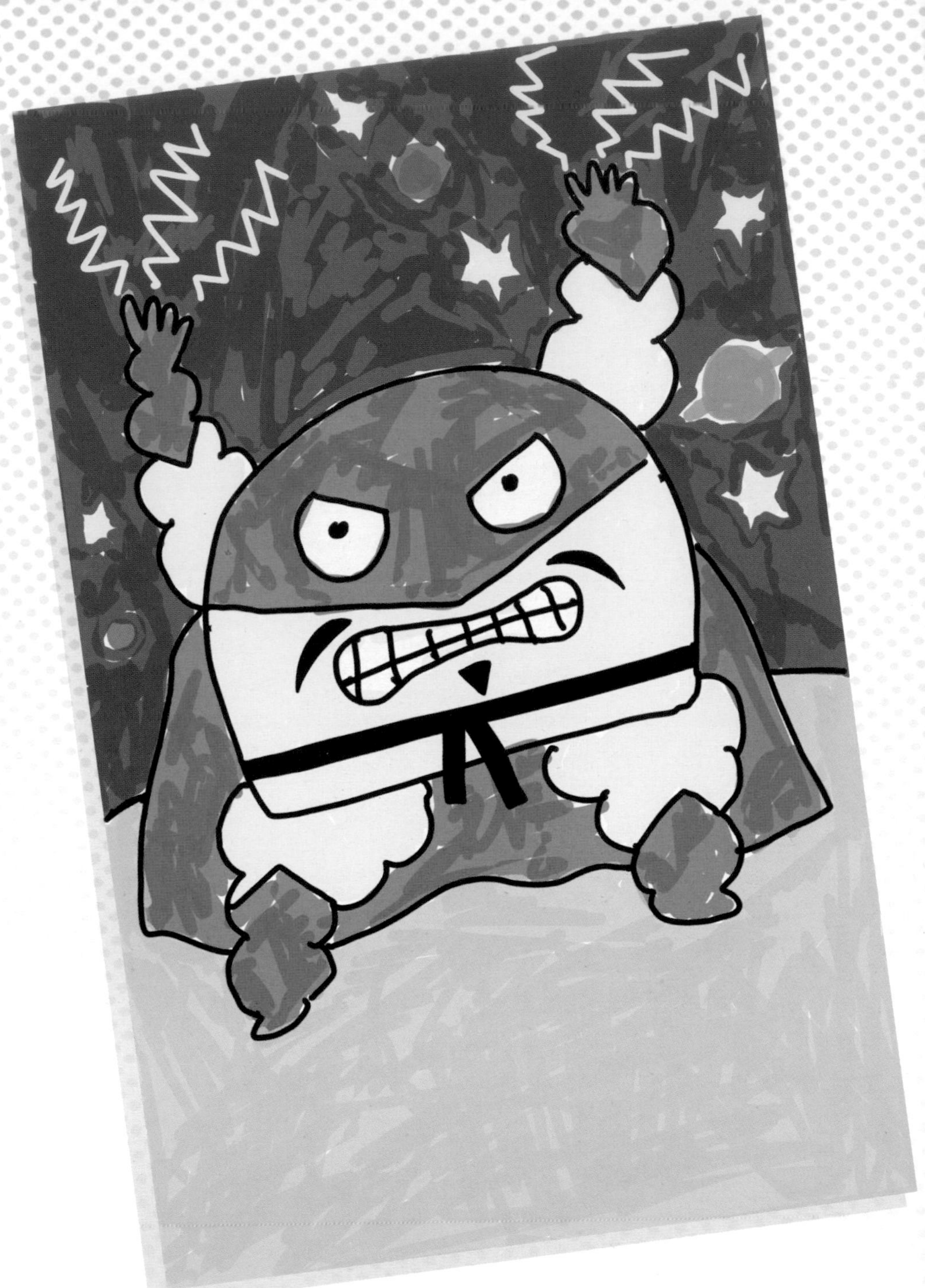

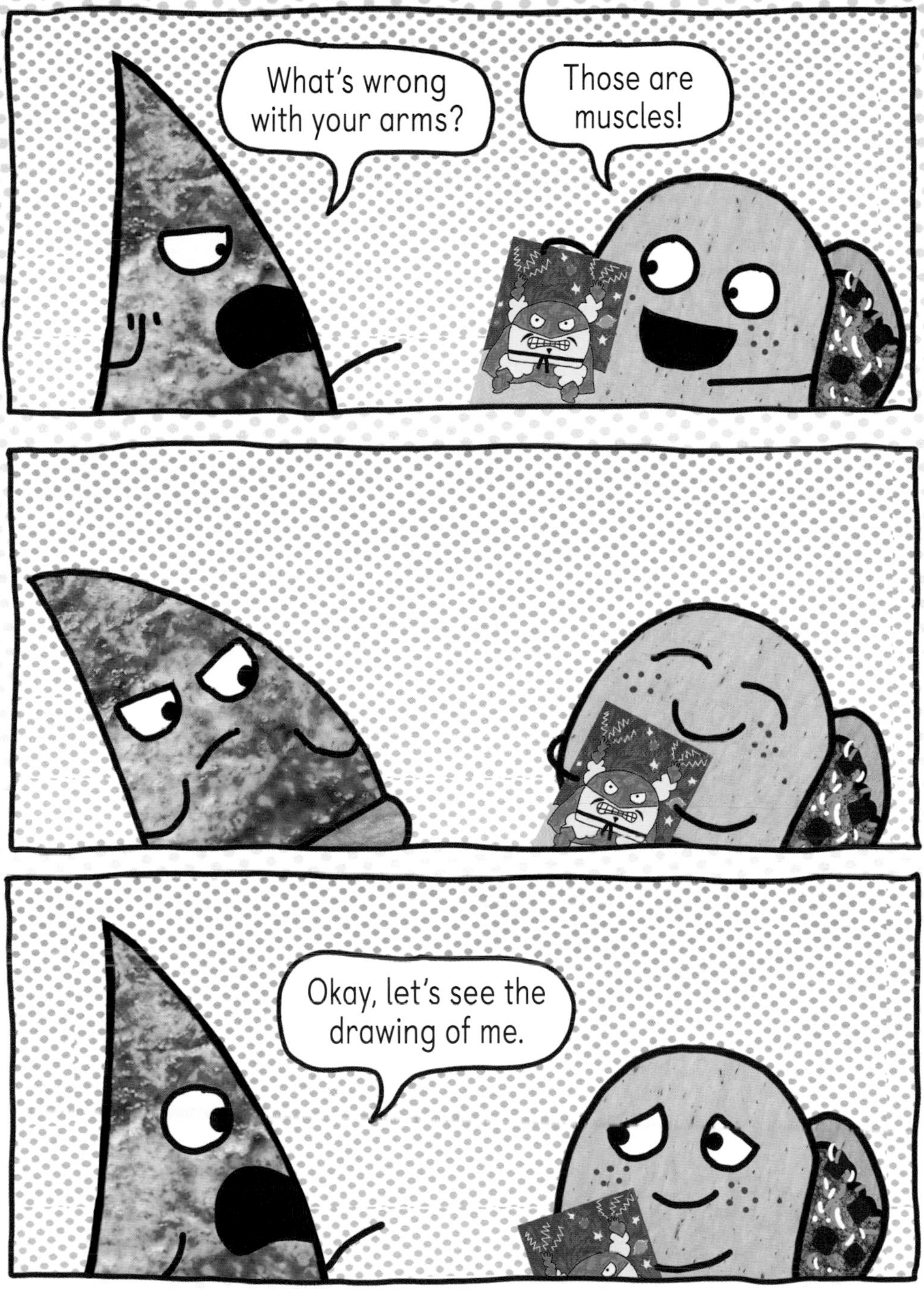
What's wrong with your arms?
Those are muscles!
Okay, let's see the drawing of me.

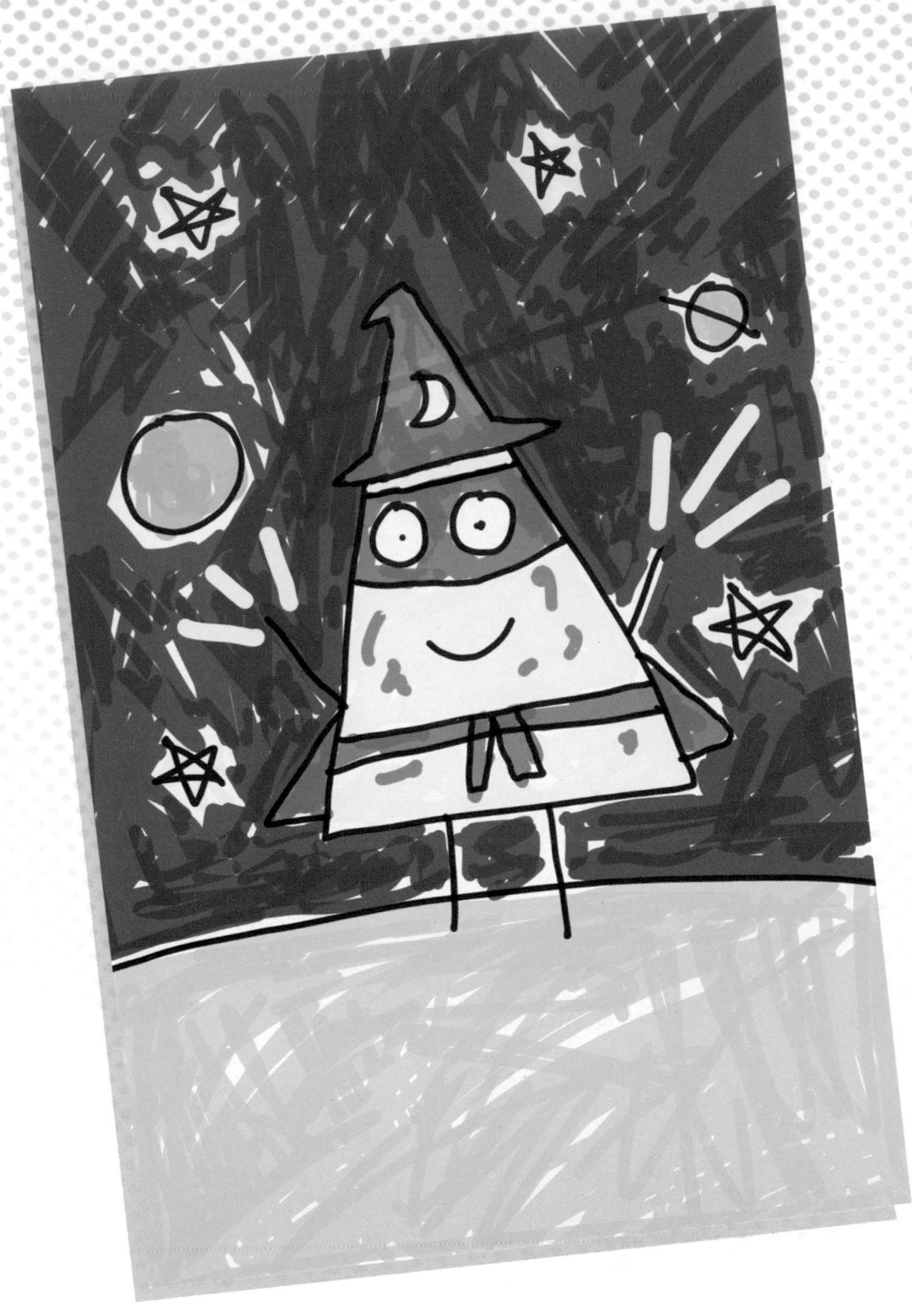

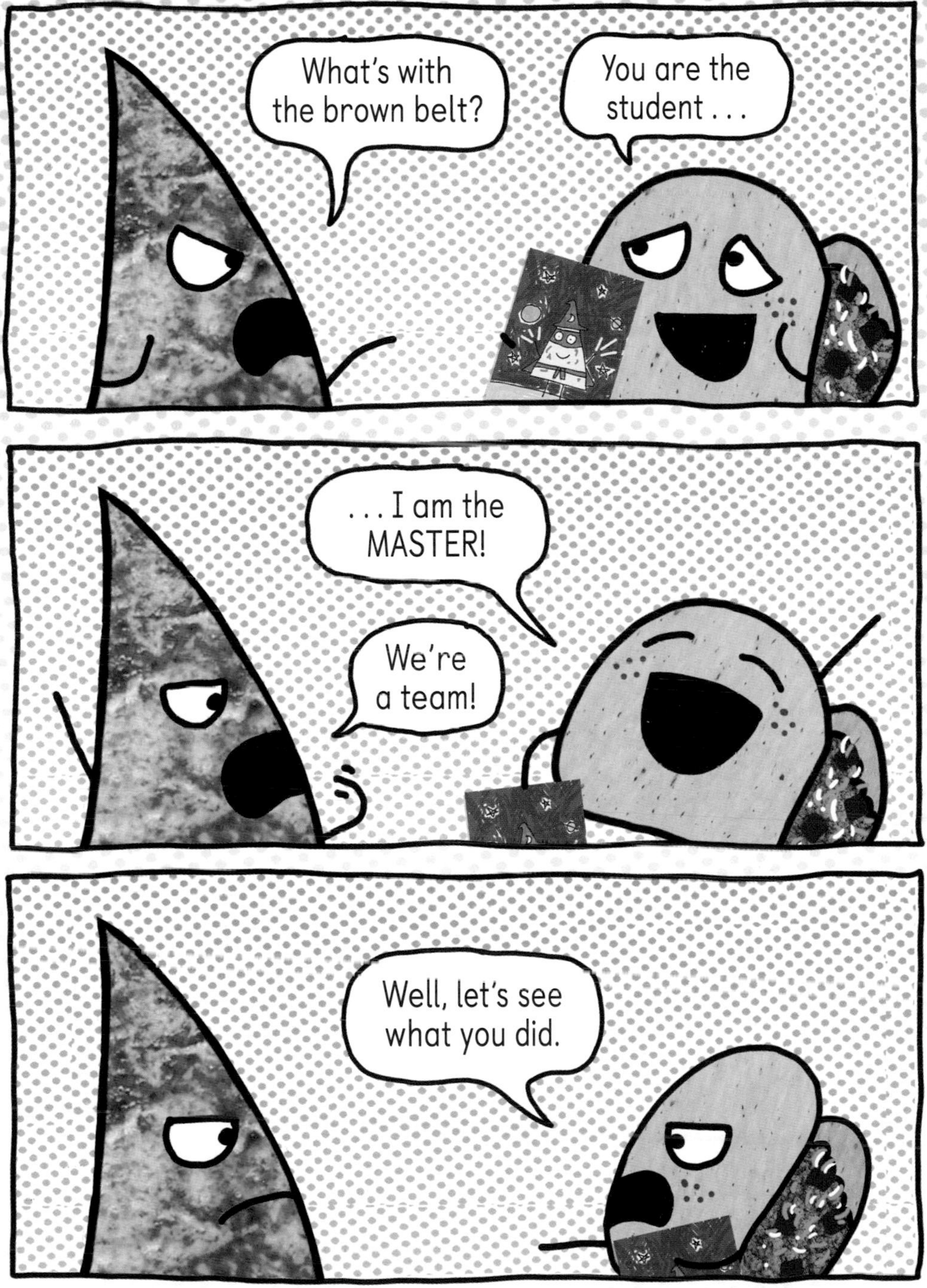
What's with the brown belt?
You are the student . . .
. . . I am the MASTER!
We're a team!
Well, let's see what you did.

TACO AWESOME

Superhero name: Taco Awesome

Real name: Taco

Age: 99

Height: 5 ft.

Superpowers: Flying, onion breath, super farts

Spells: Bright lights

Weakness: spiders

Origins: From planet Taco

Works at a bank. Born super.

Part of The SUPER-AWESOME TEAM!

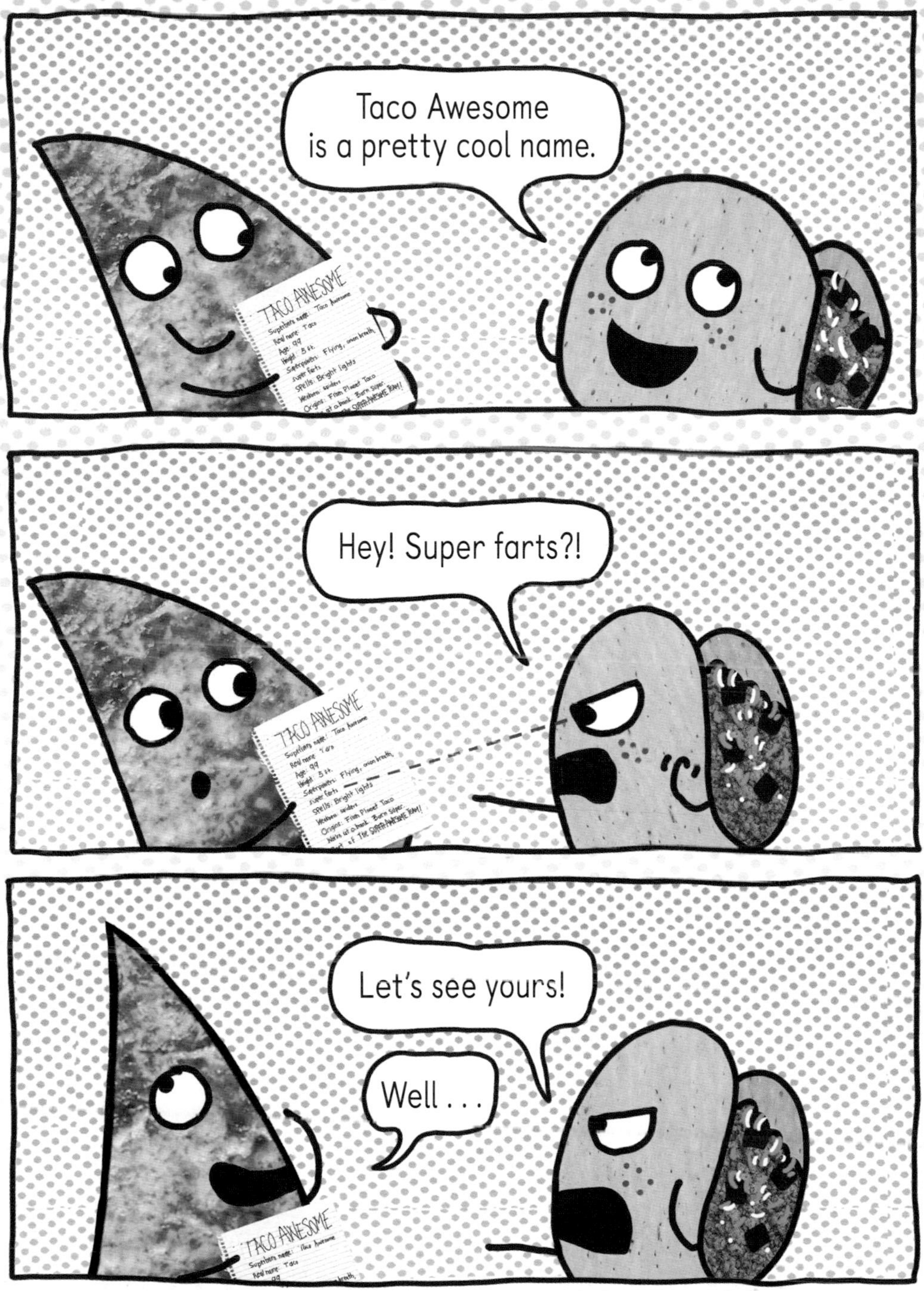

Taco Awesome is a pretty cool name.
TACO AWESOME
Hey! Super farts?!
TACO AWESOME
Let's see yours!
Well . . .
TACO AWESOME

SUPER SLICE

Superhero name: Super Slice

Real name: Pizza

Age: 100

Height: 10 ft.

Superpowers: Flying, super everything

Spells: Mind tricks

Weakness: Modesty

Origins: King of planet Pizza Born Pizza Supreme. Part of THE SUPER-AWESOME TEAM.

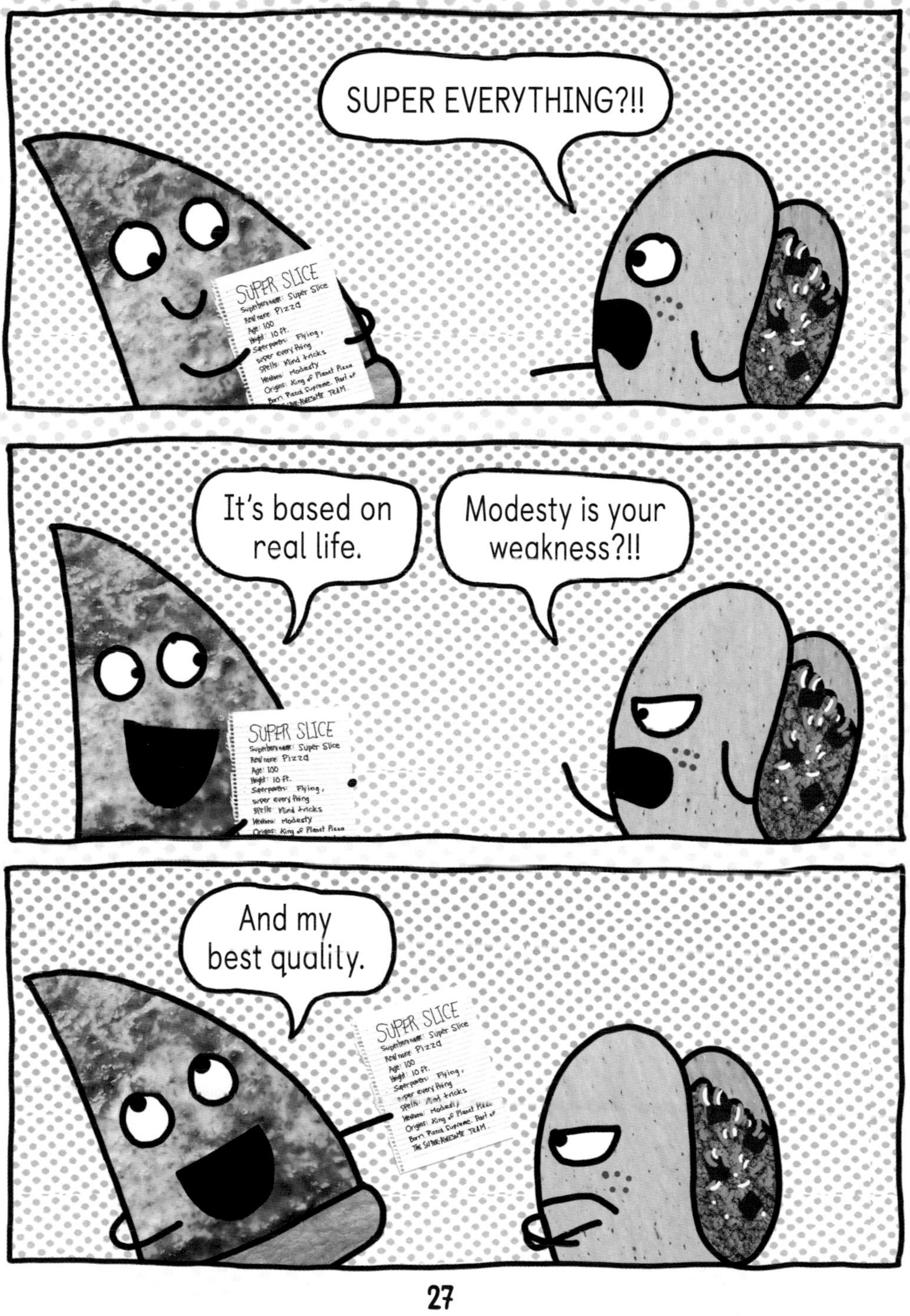
SUPER EVERYTHING?!!
SUPER SLICE
It's based on real life.
Modesty is your weakness?!!
SUPER SLICE
And my best quality.
SUPER SLICE

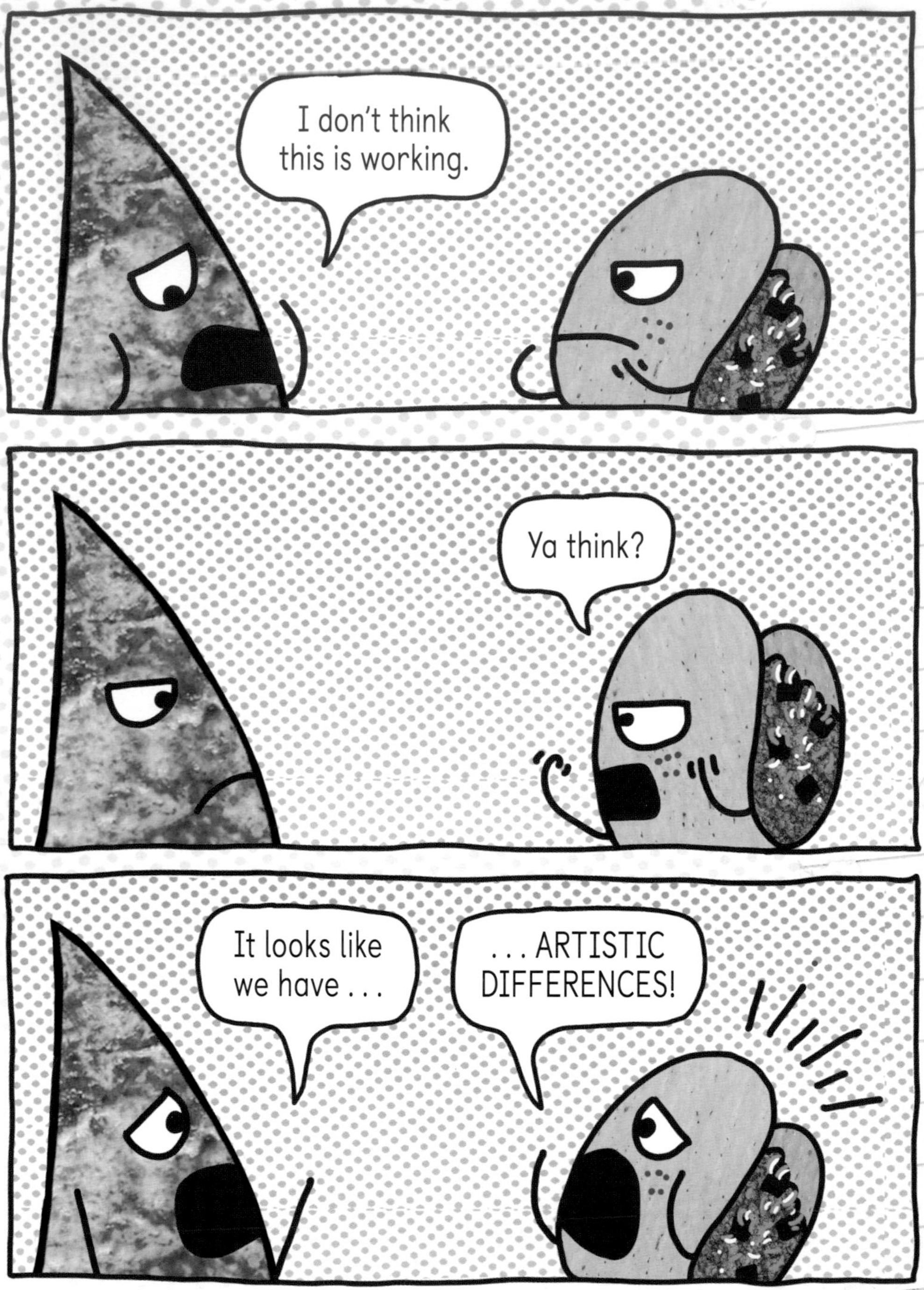
I don't think this is working.
Ya think?
It looks like we have . . .
. . . ARTISTIC DIFFERENCES!

Chapter 4
Pizza and Taco Have Artistic Differences

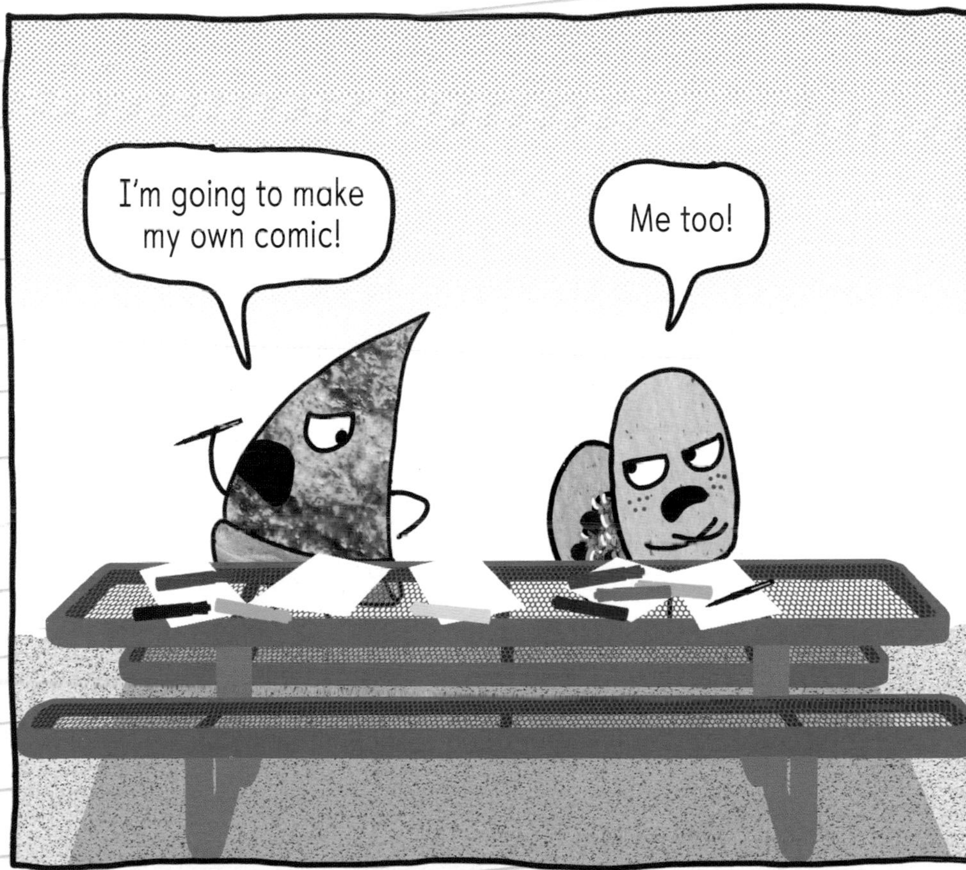
I'm going to make my own comic!
Me too!

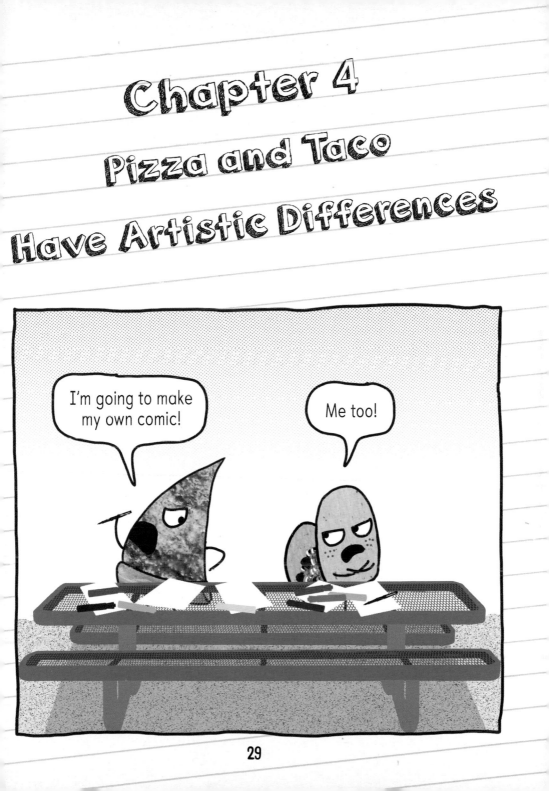

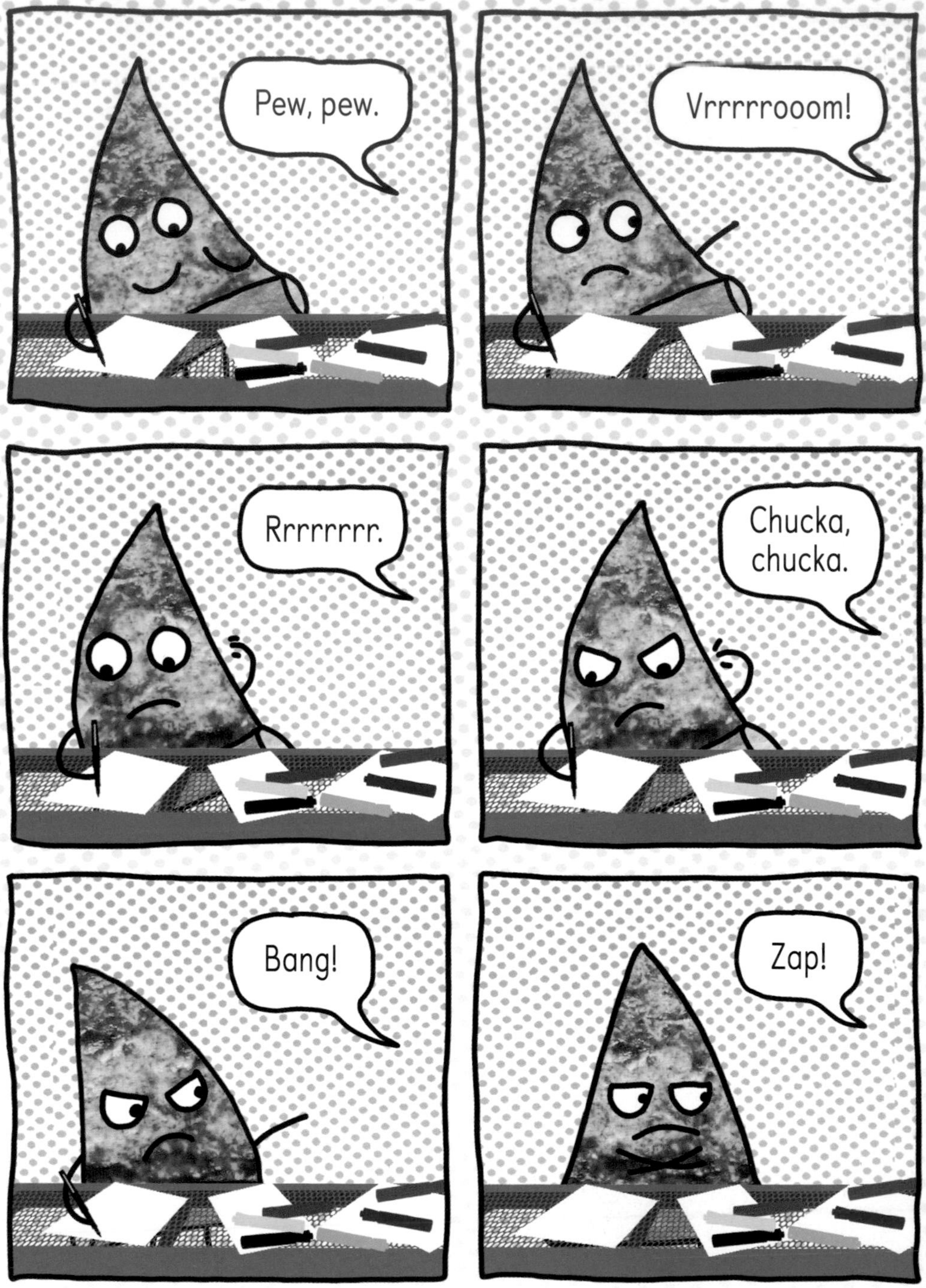
Pew, pew.
Vrrrrrooom!
Rrrrrrrr.
Chucka, chucka.
Bang!
Zap!

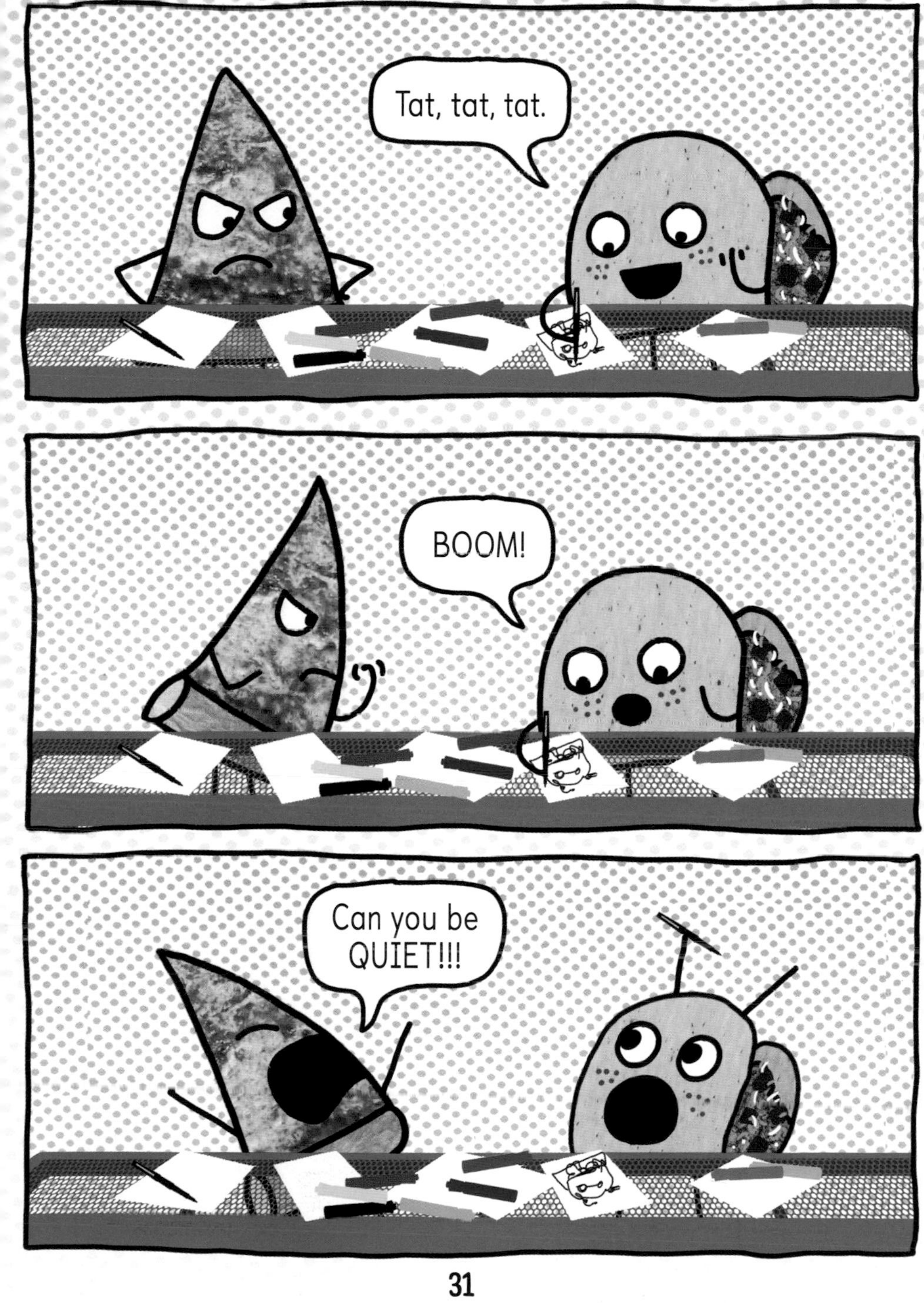
Tat, tat, tat.
BOOM!
Can you be QUIET!!!

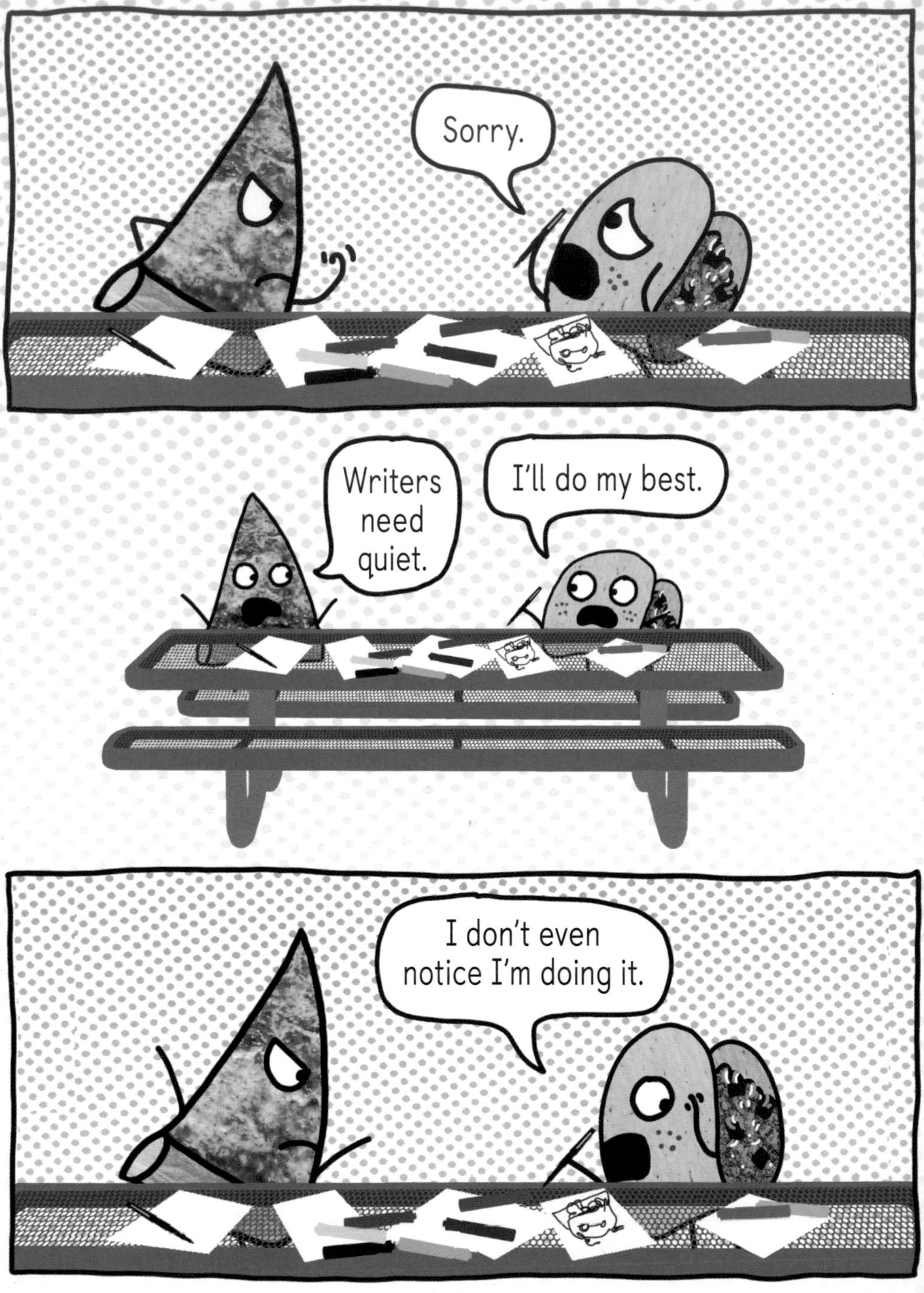

Sorry.
Writers need quiet.
I'll do my best.
I don't even notice I'm doing it.

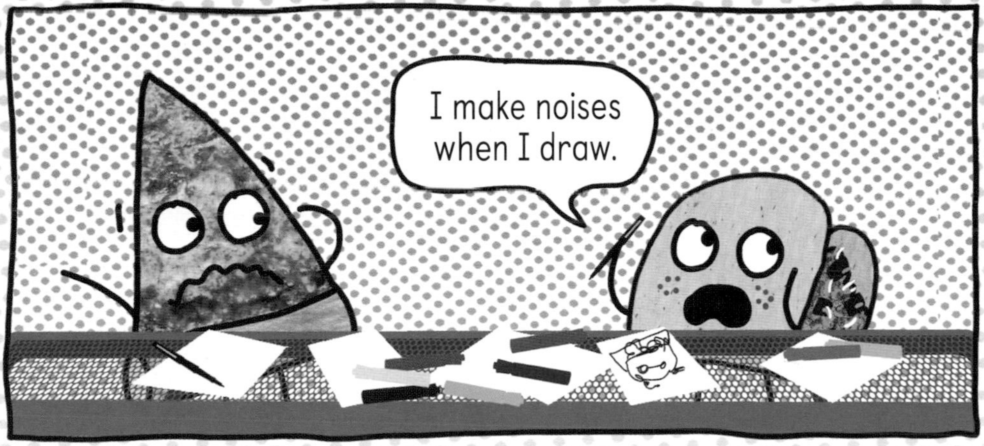
I make noises when I draw.

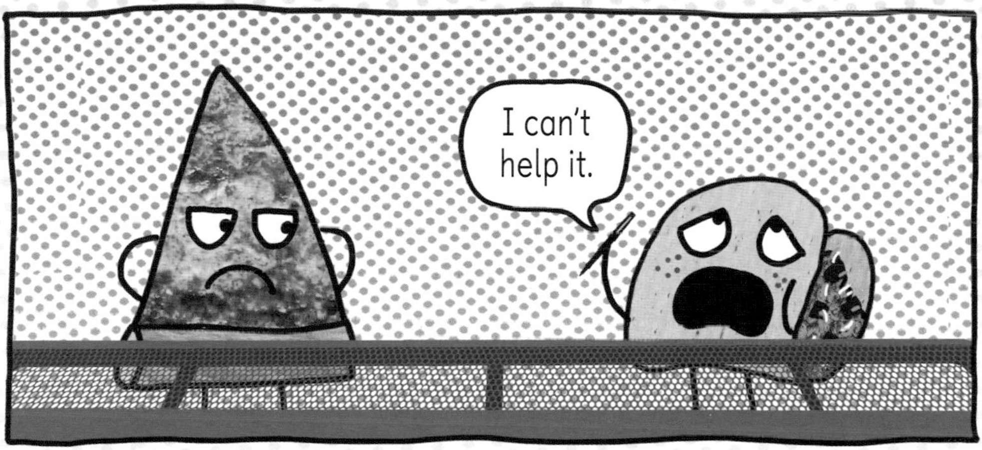
I can't help it.

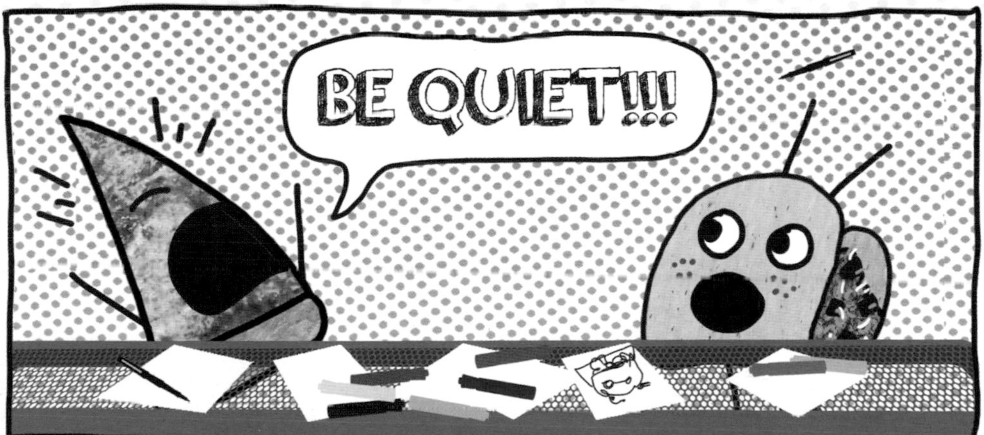
BE QUIET!!!

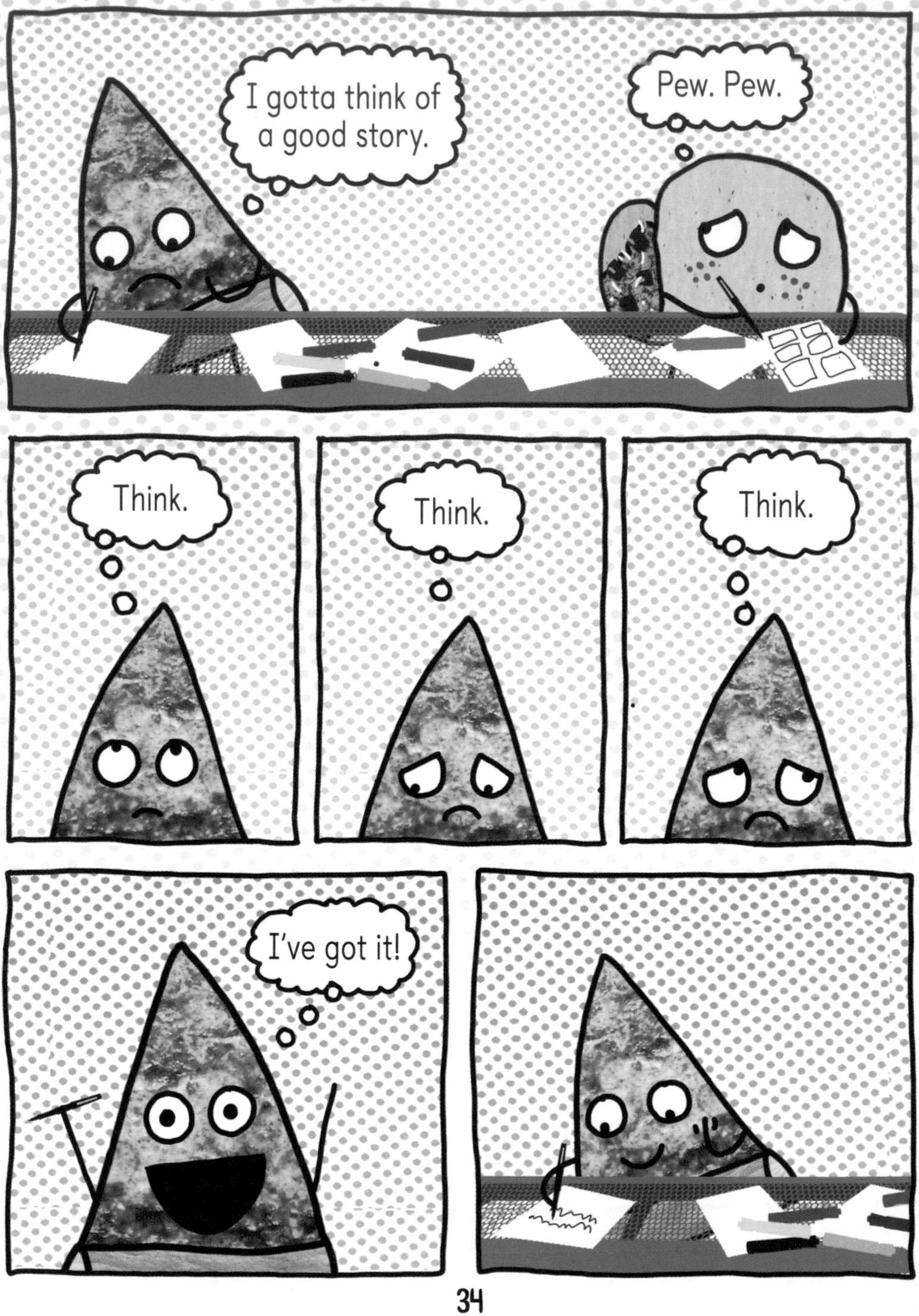

I gotta think of a good story.
Pew. Pew.
Think.
Think.
Think.
I've got it!

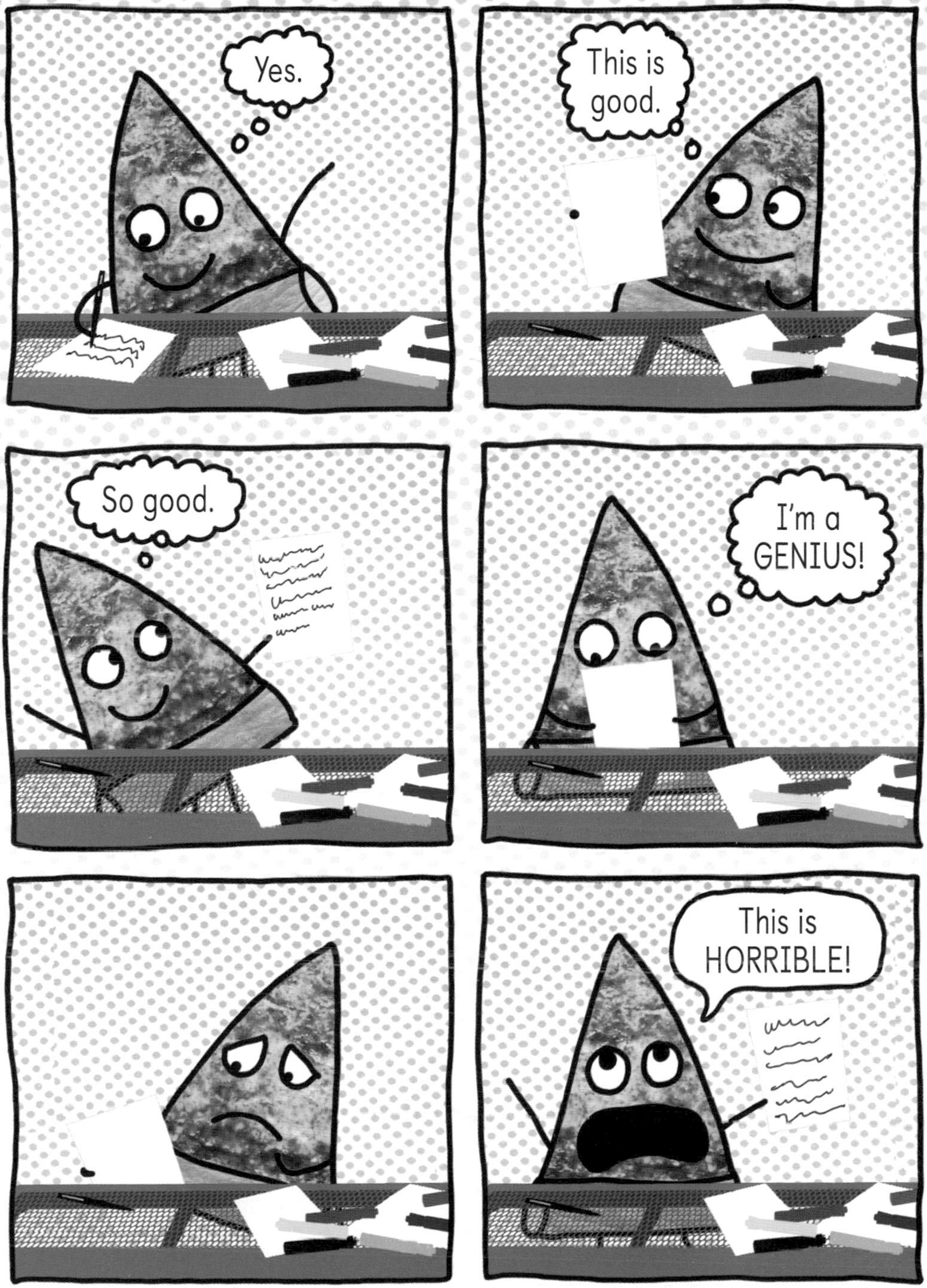
Yes.
This is good.
So good.
I'm a GENIUS!
This is HORRIBLE!

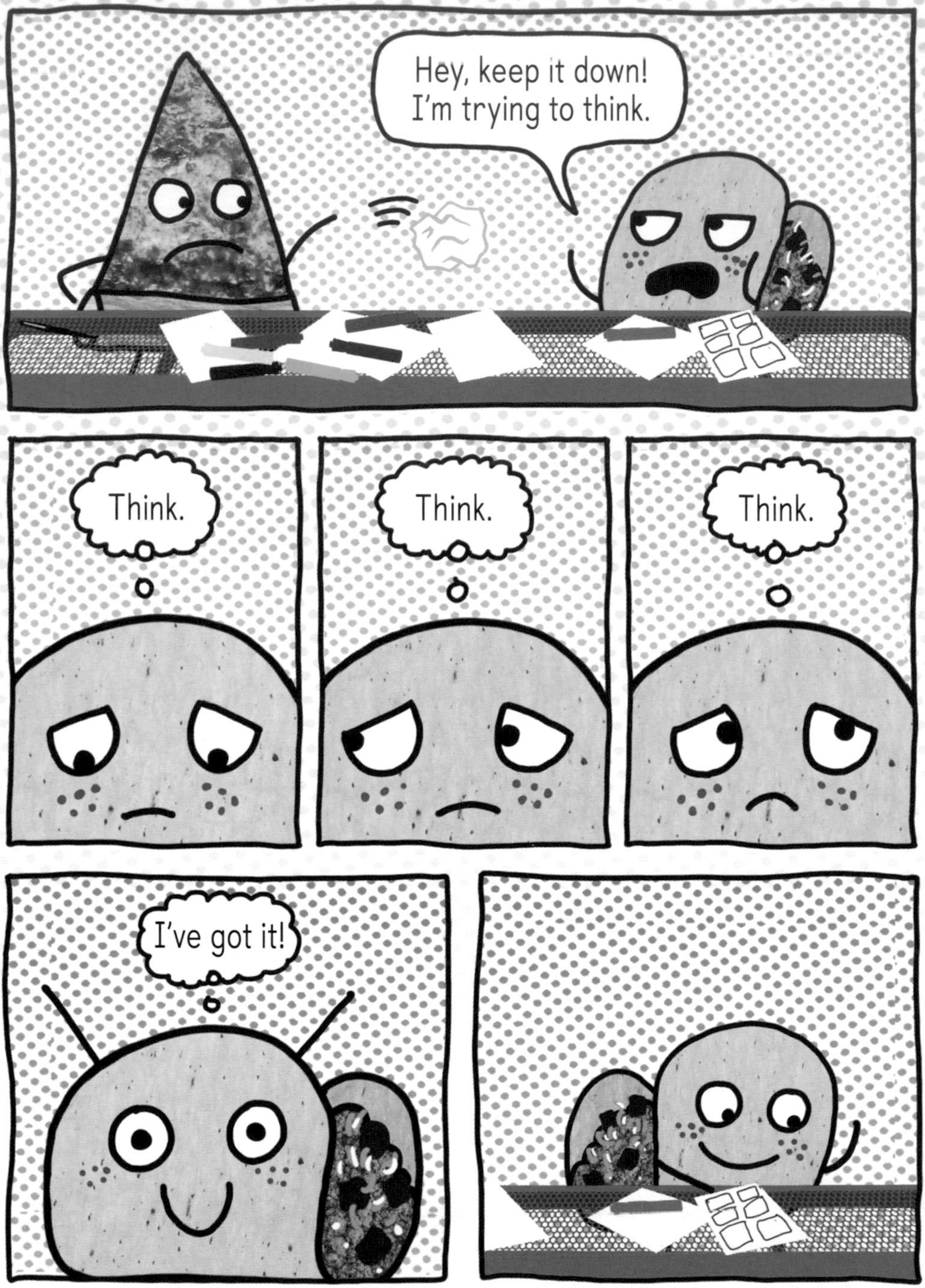
Hey, keep it down!
I'm trying to think.
Think.
Think.
Think.
I've got it!

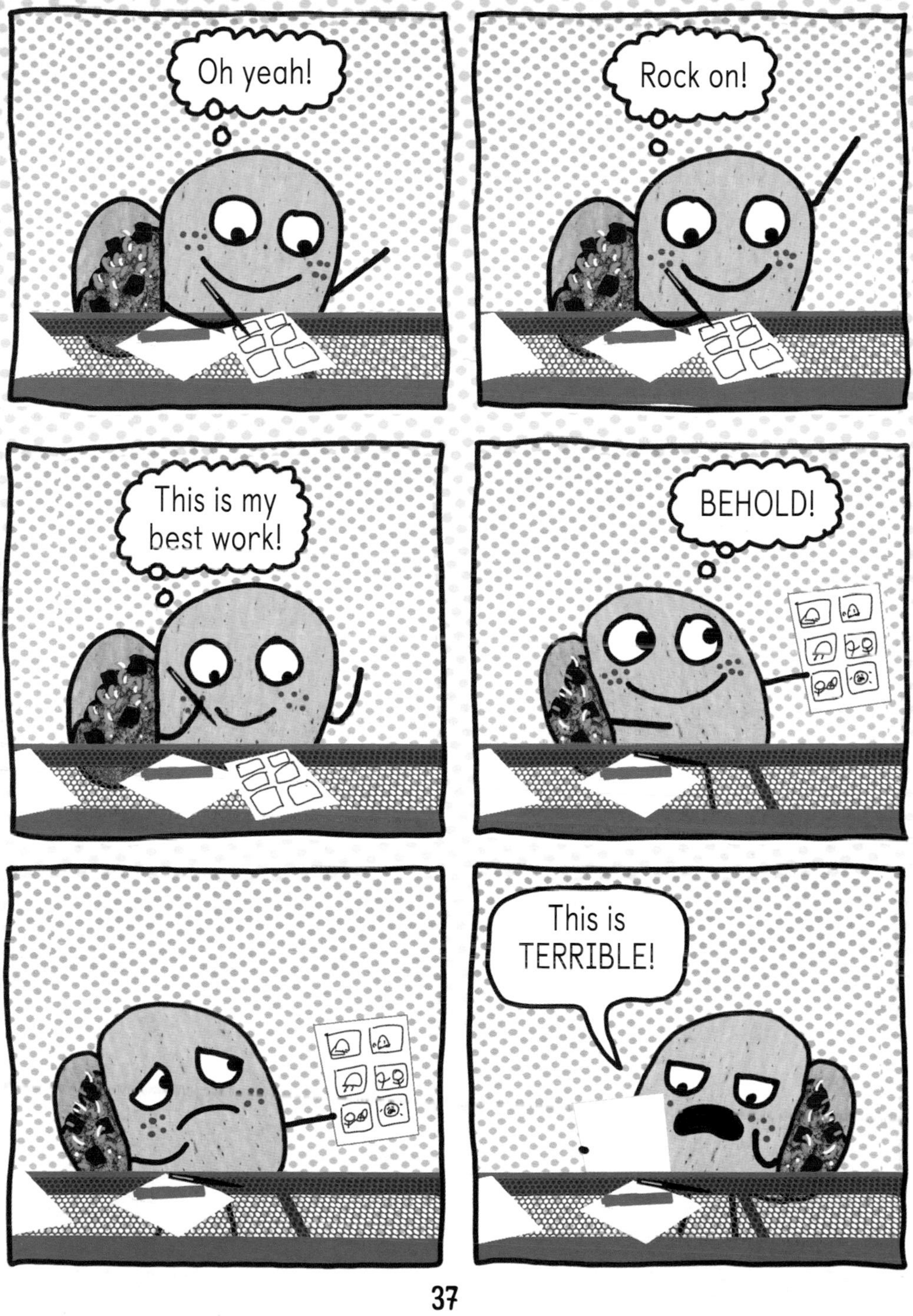
Oh yeah!
Rock on!
This is my best work!
BEHOLD!
This is TERRIBLE!

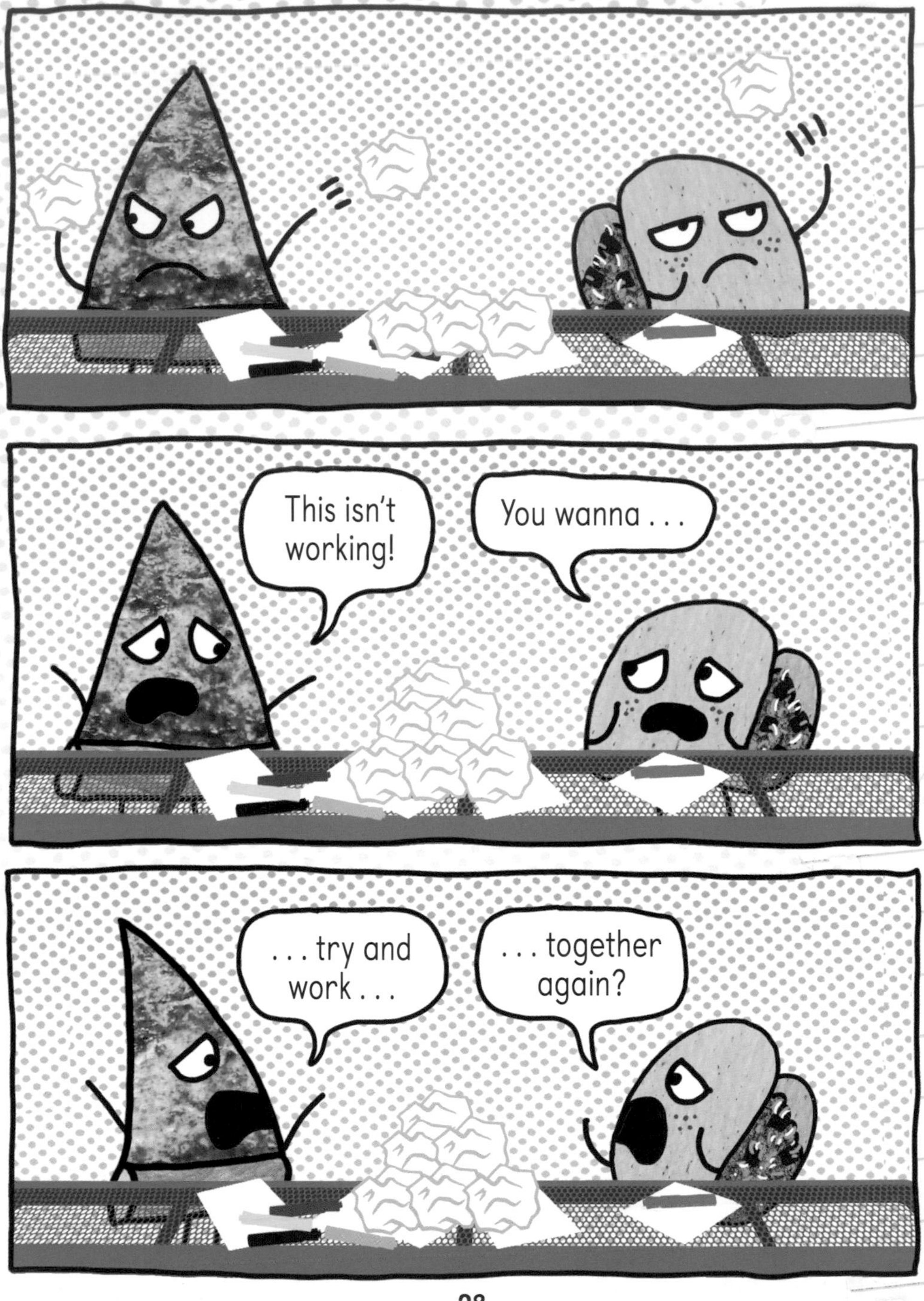
This isn't working!
You wanna . . .
. . . try and work . . .
. . . together again?

Chapter 5
Pizza and Taco Together Again!

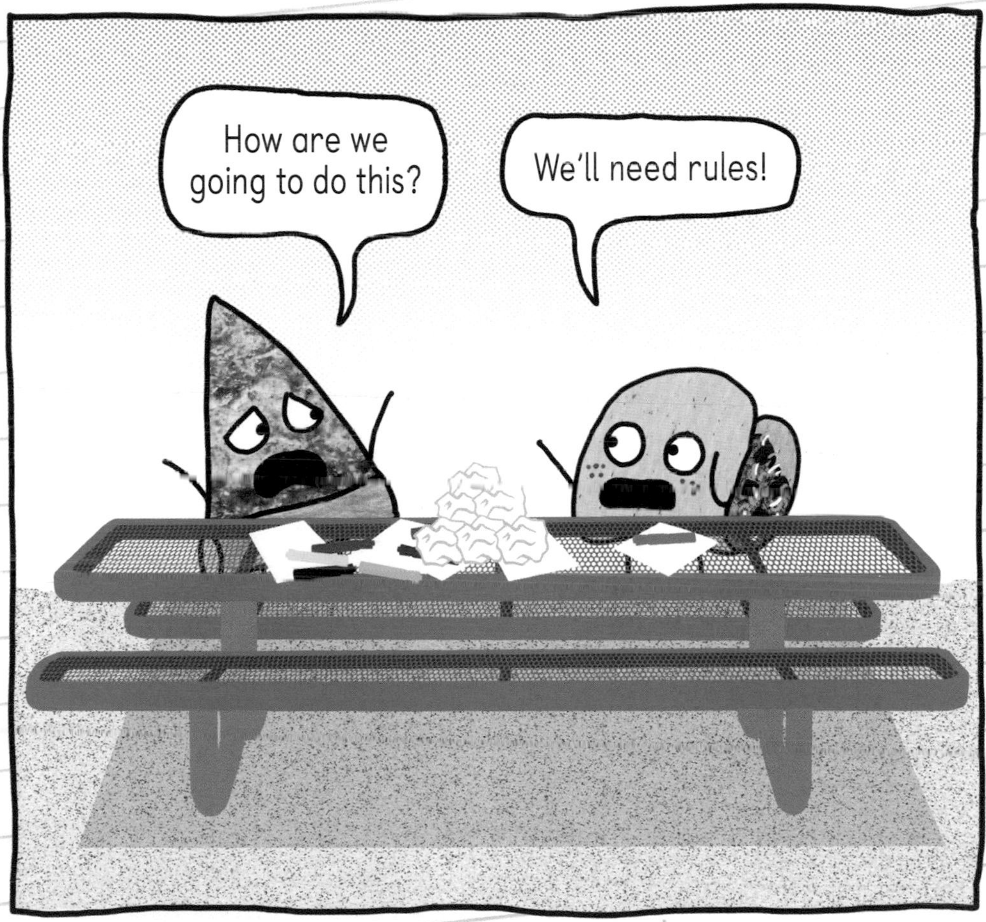
How are we going to do this?
We'll need rules!

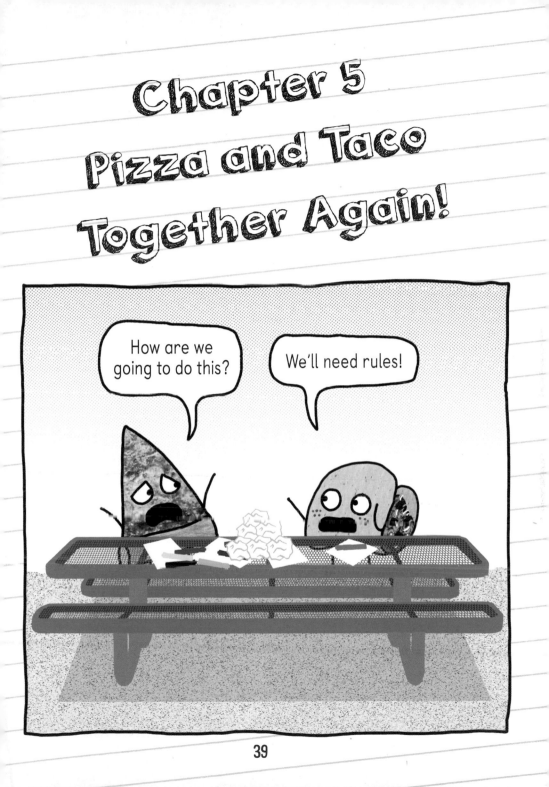

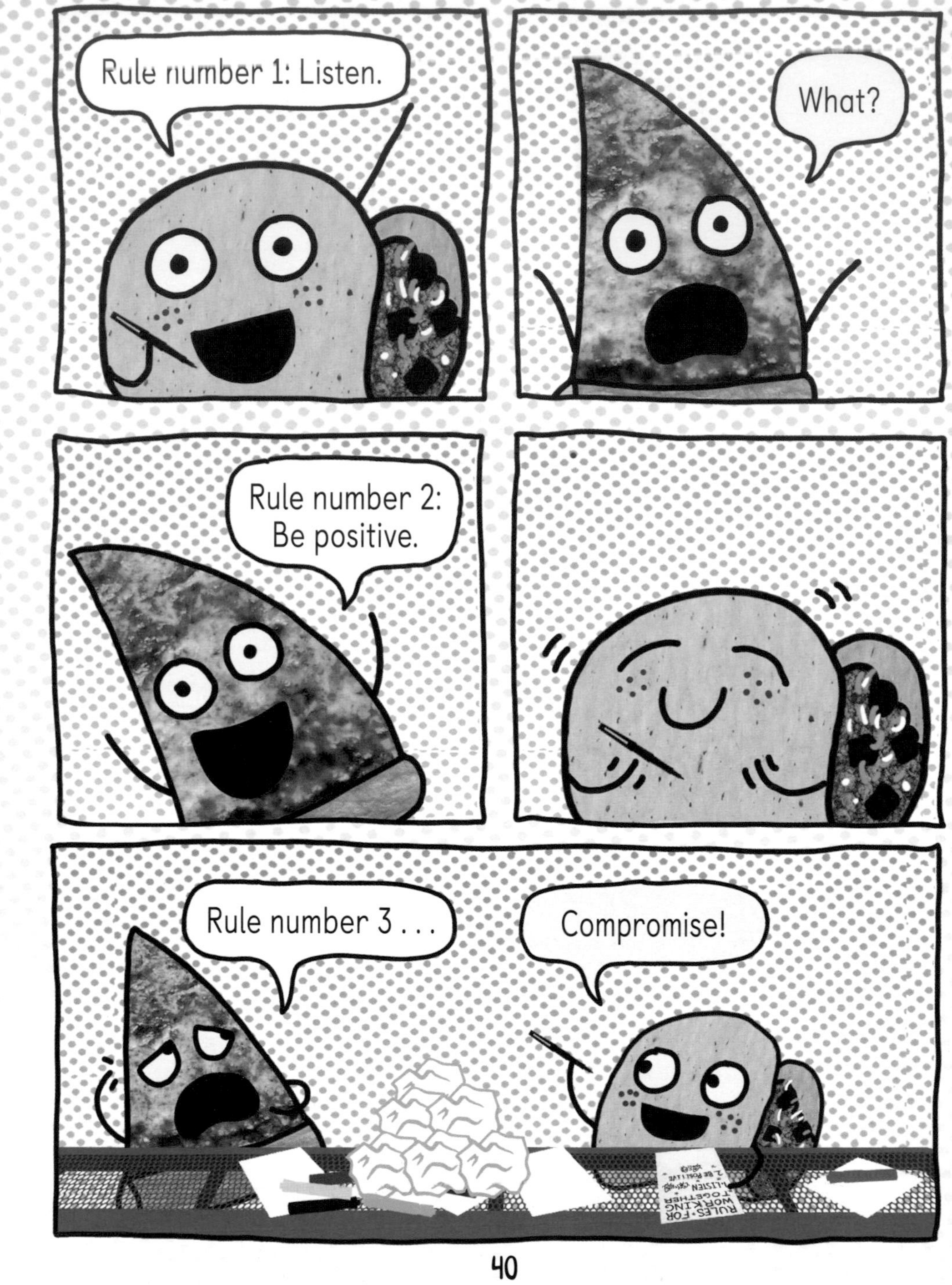
Rule number 1: Listen.
What?
Rule number 2: Be positive.
Rule number 3 . . .
Compromise!

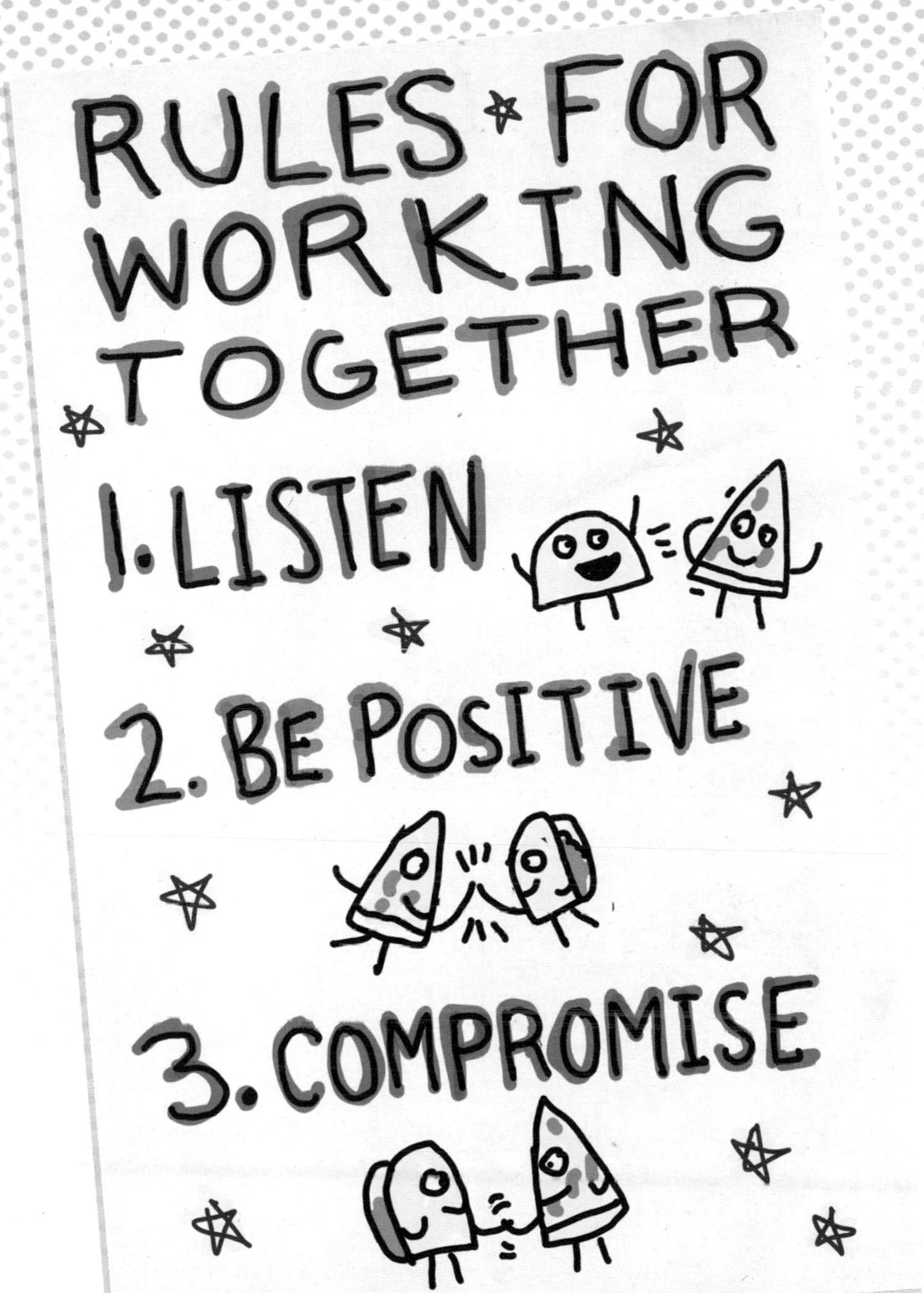
RULES FOR WORKING TOGETHER
1. LISTEN
2. BE POSITIVE
3. COMPROMISE

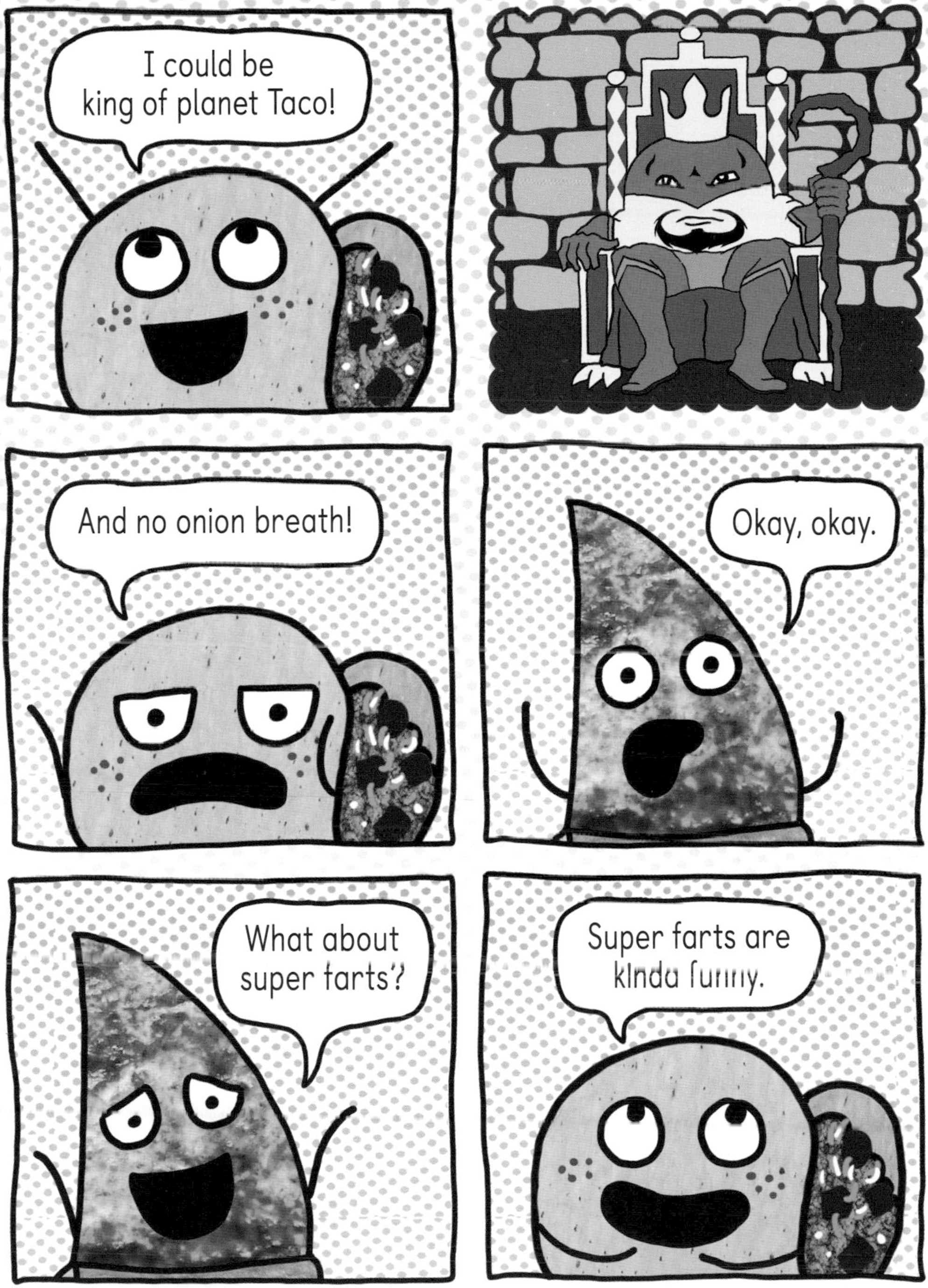
I could be king of planet Taco!
And no onion breath!
Okay, okay.
What about super farts?
Super farts are kinda funny.

44

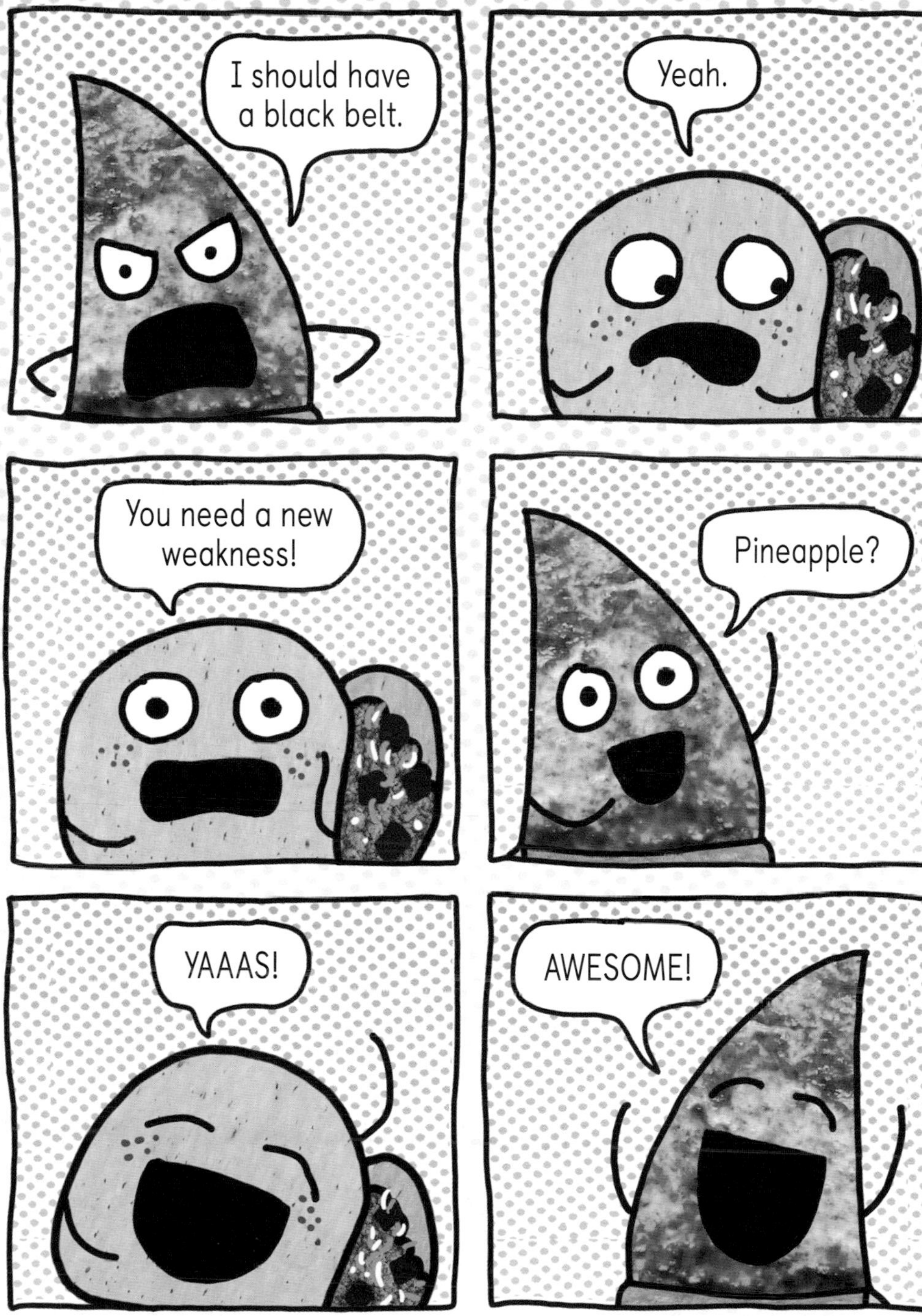
I should have a black belt.
Yeah.
You need a new weakness!
Pineapple?
YAAAS!
AWESOME!

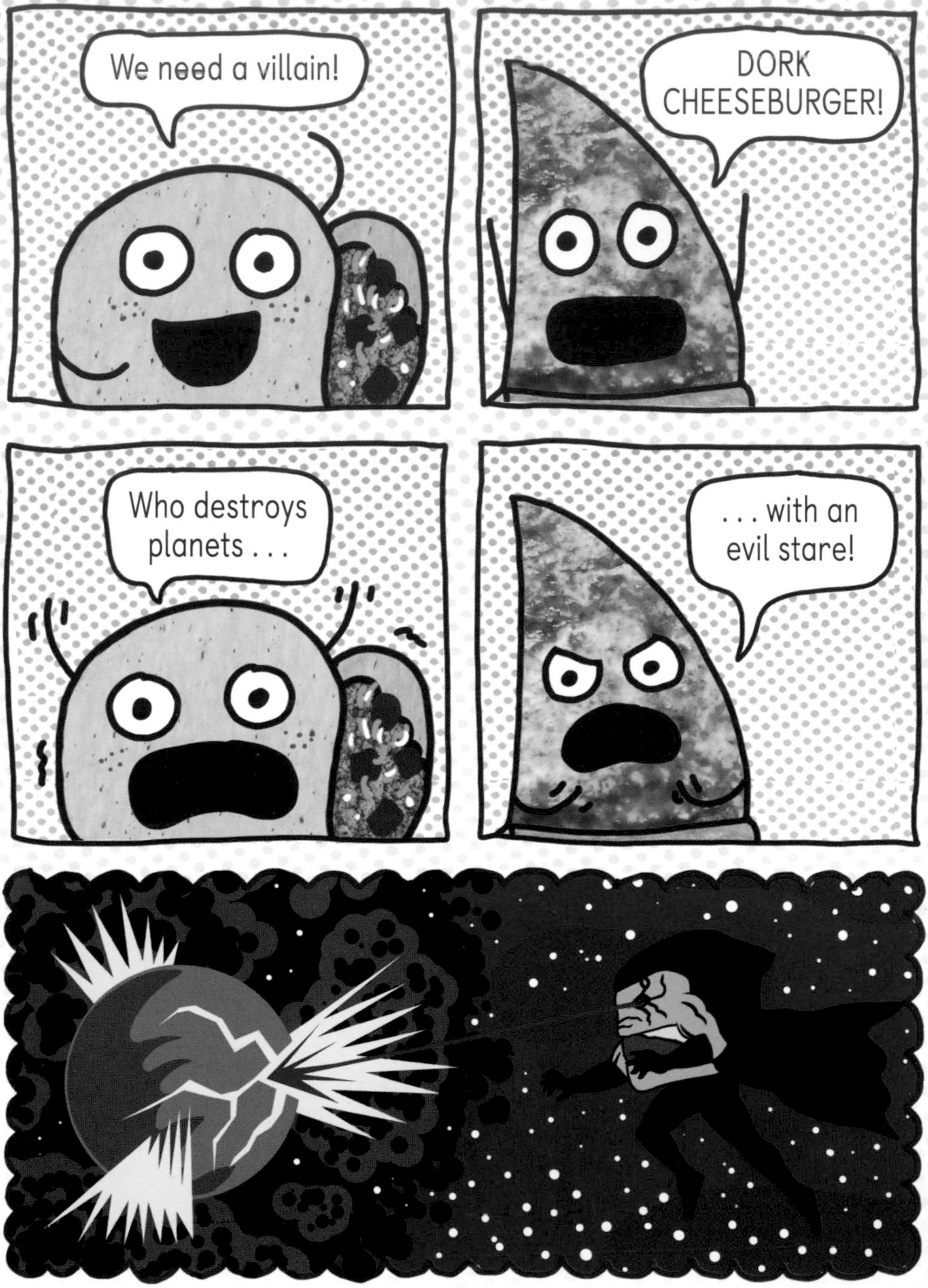
We need a villain!
DORK CHEESEBURGER!
Who destroys planets . . .
. . . with an evil stare!

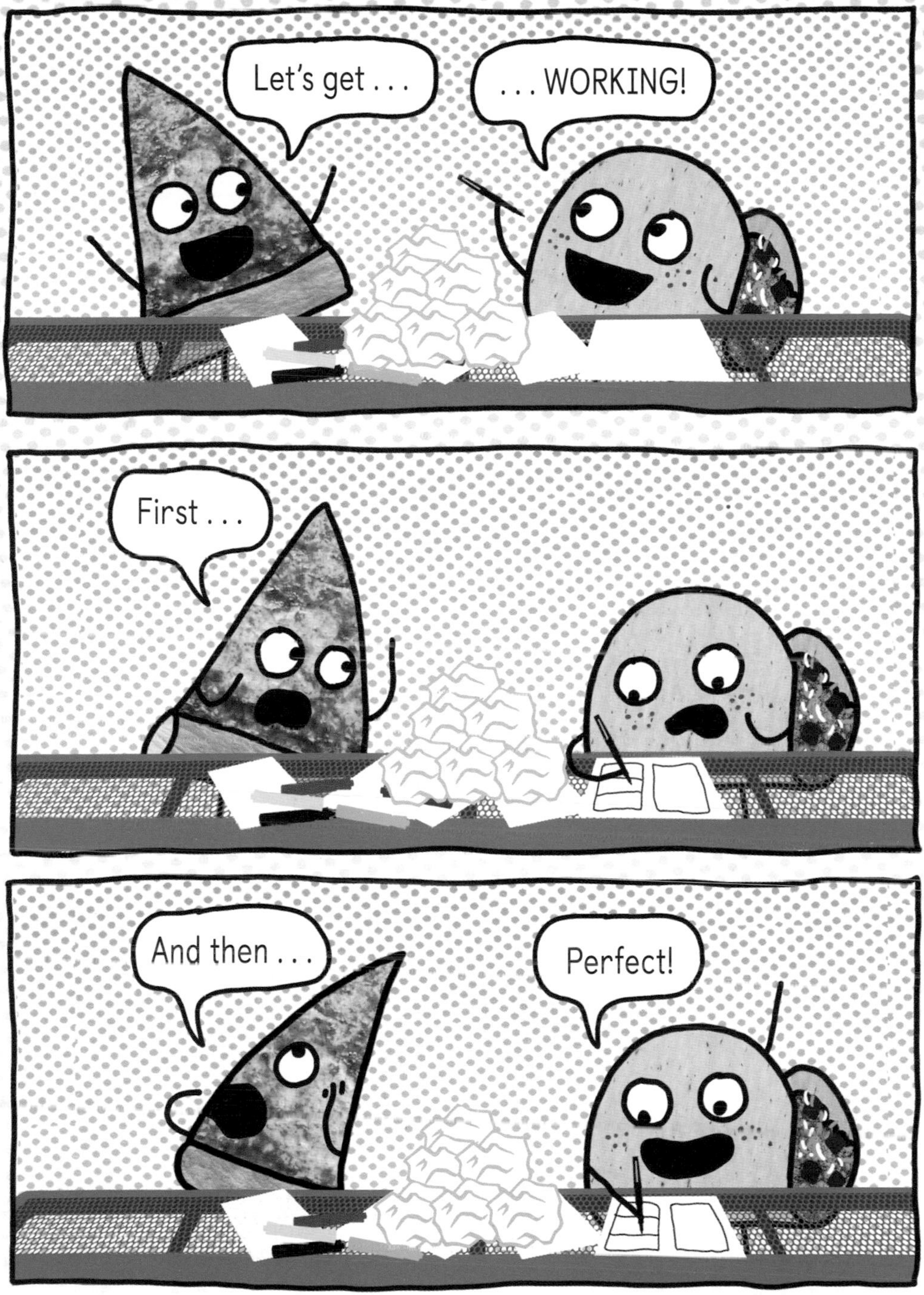
Let's get . . .
. . . WORKING!
First . . .
And then . . .
Perfect!

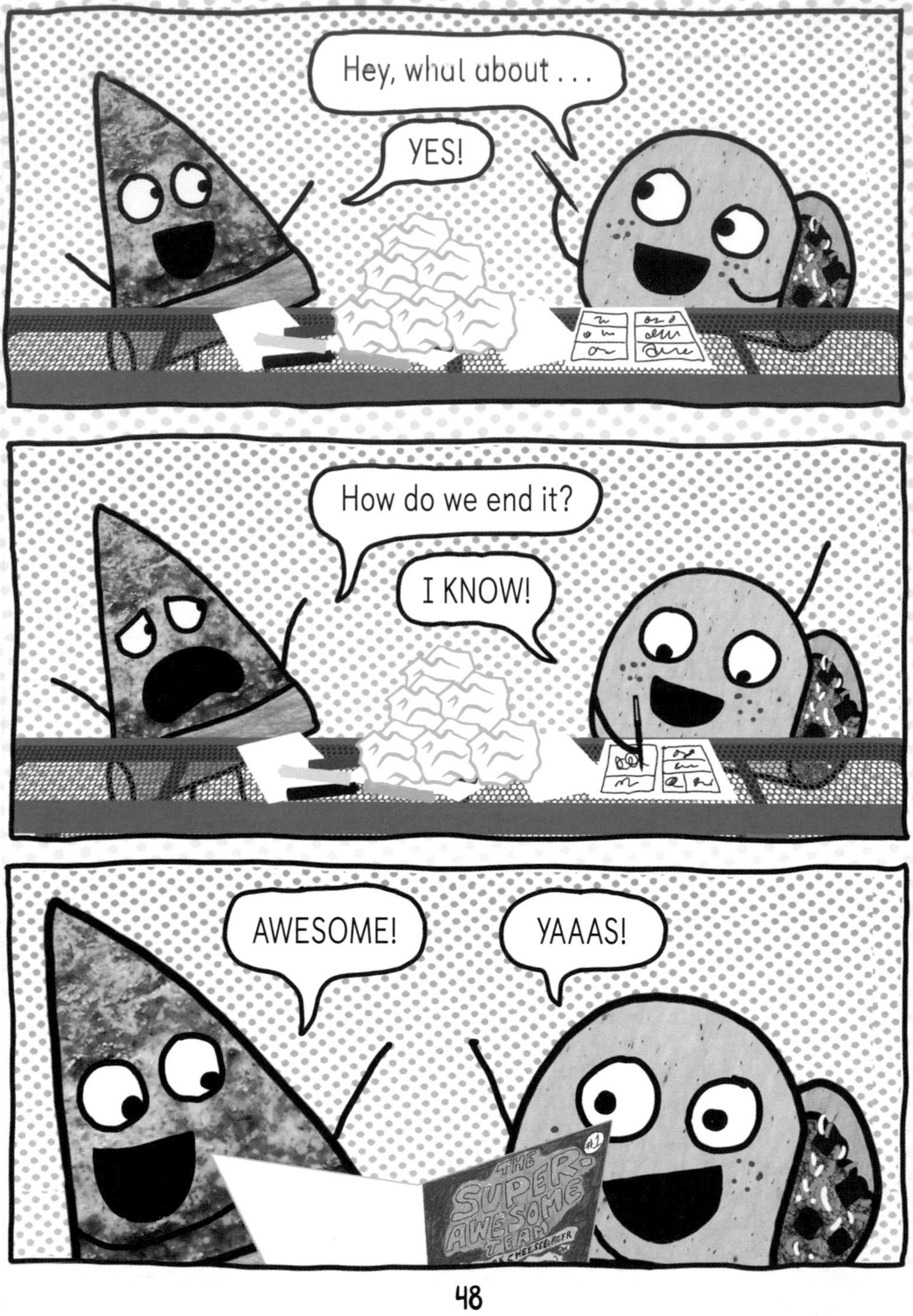
Hey, what about . . .
YES!
How do we end it?
I KNOW!
AWESOME!
YAAAS!
#1
THE SUPER-AWESOME TEAM

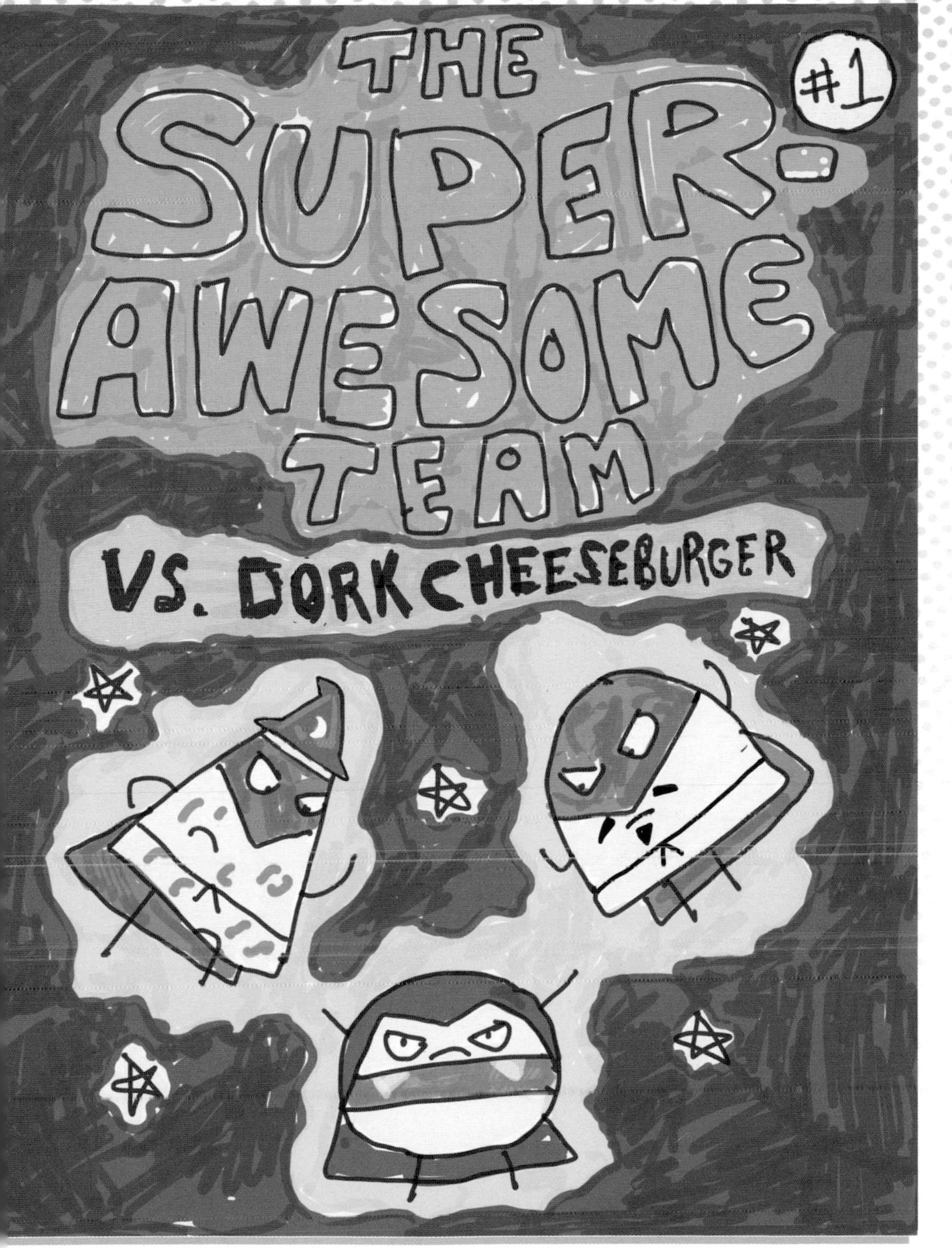
THE SUPER-AWESOME TEAM
#1
VS. DORKCHEESEBURGER

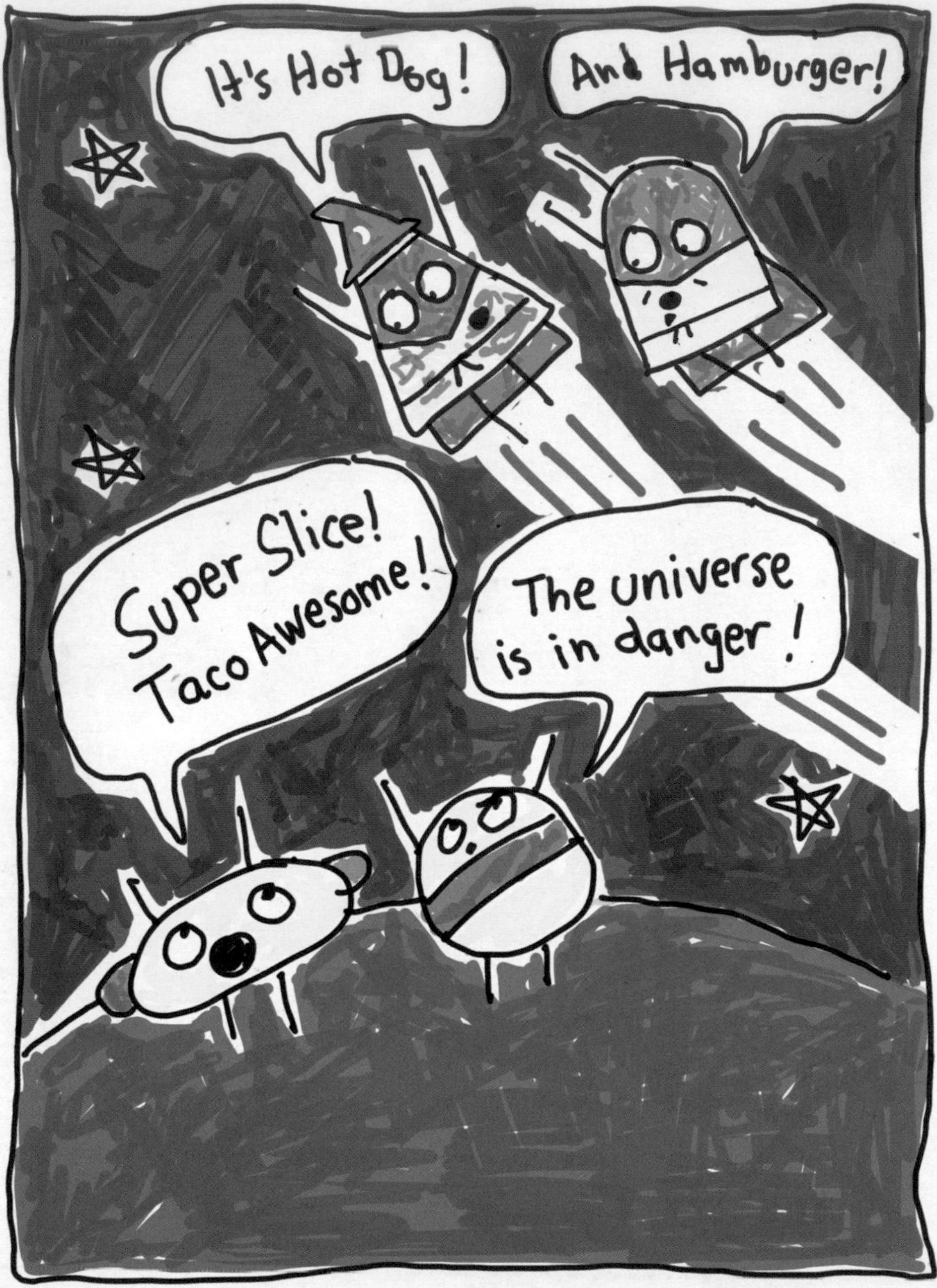
It's Hot Dog!
And Hamburger!
Super Slice! Taco Awesome!
The universe is in danger!

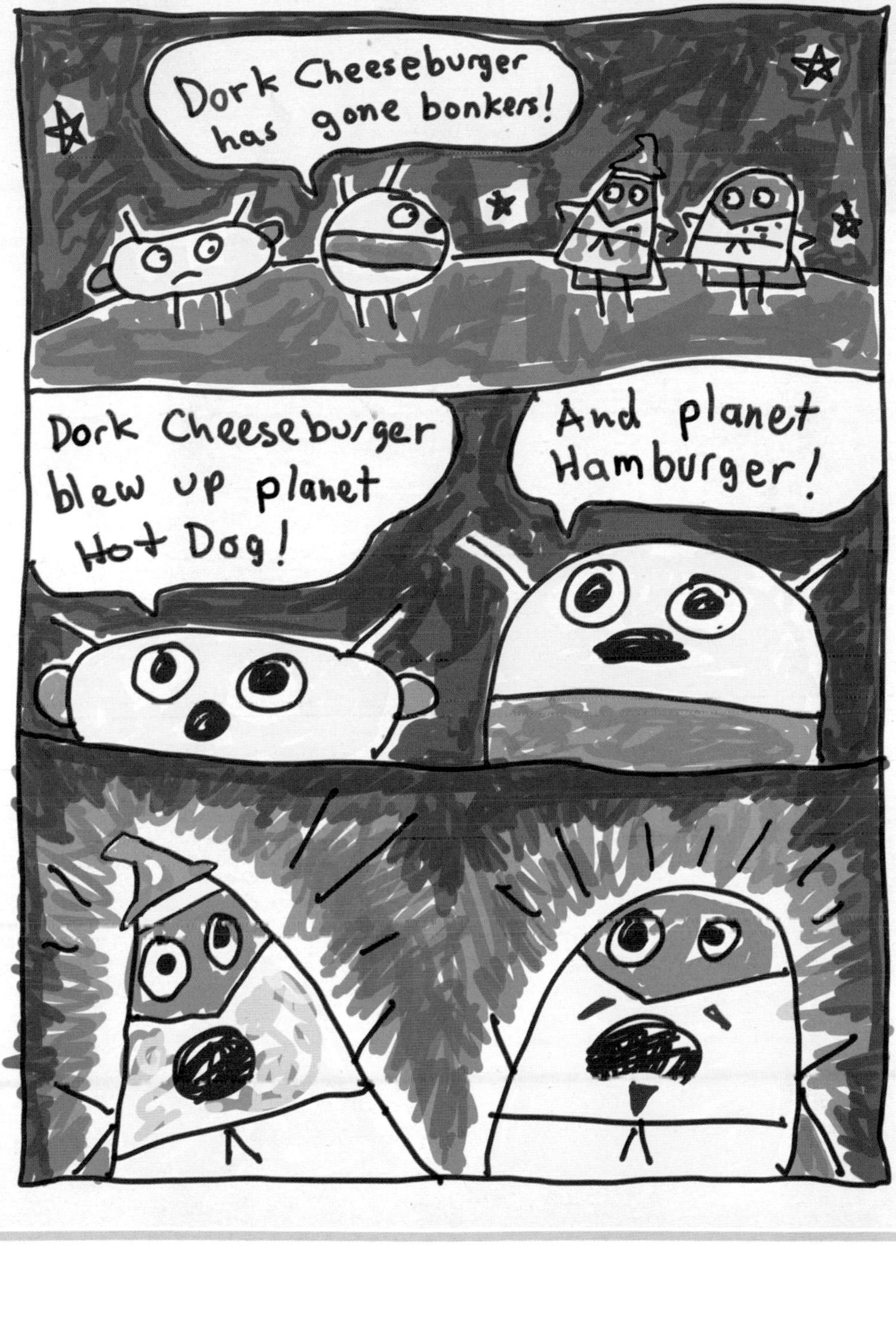
Dork Cheeseburger has gone bonkers!
Dork Cheeseburger blew up planet Hot Dog!
And planet Hamburger!

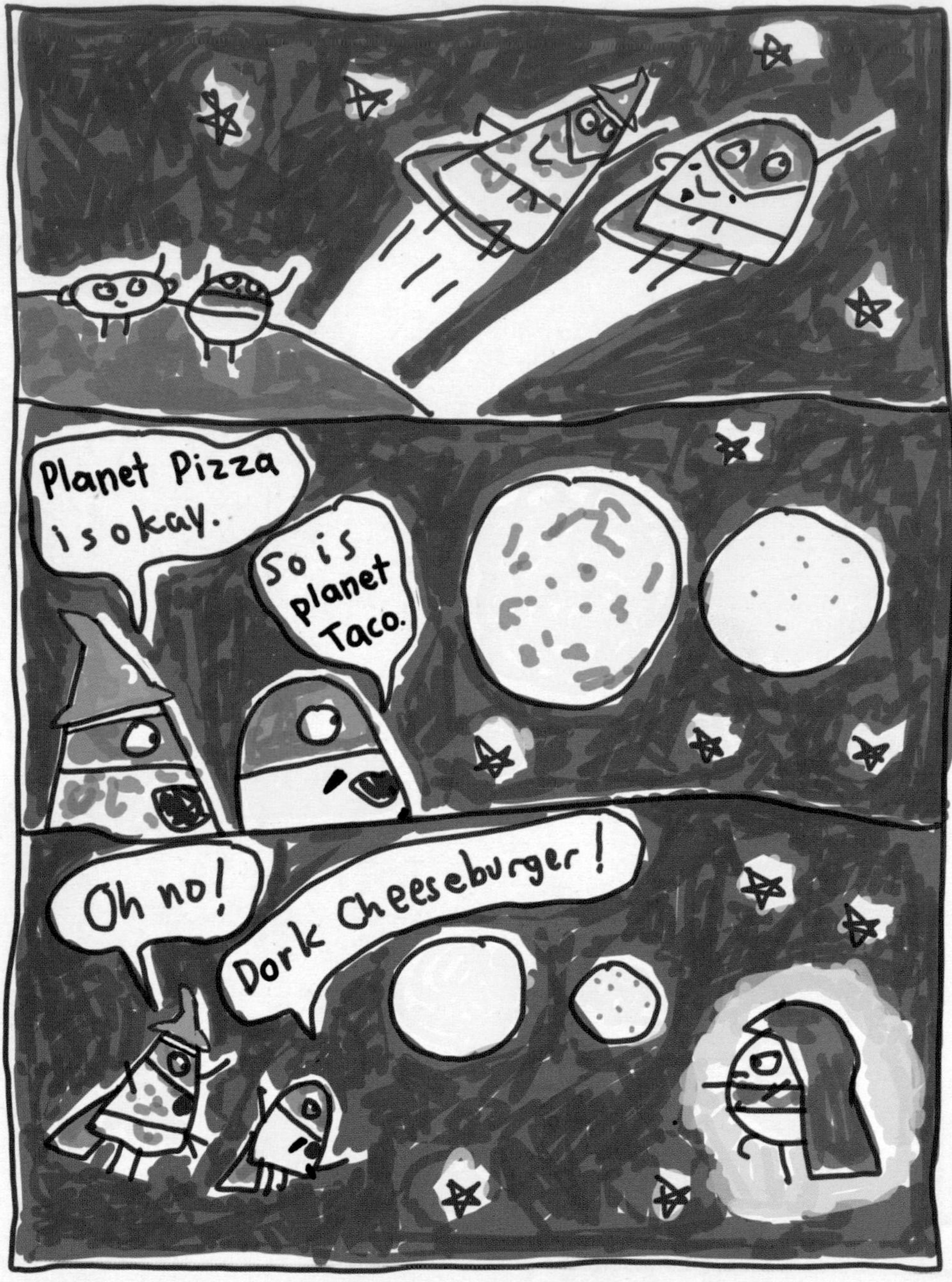
Planet Pizza is okay.
So is planet Taco.
Oh no!
Dork Cheeseburger!

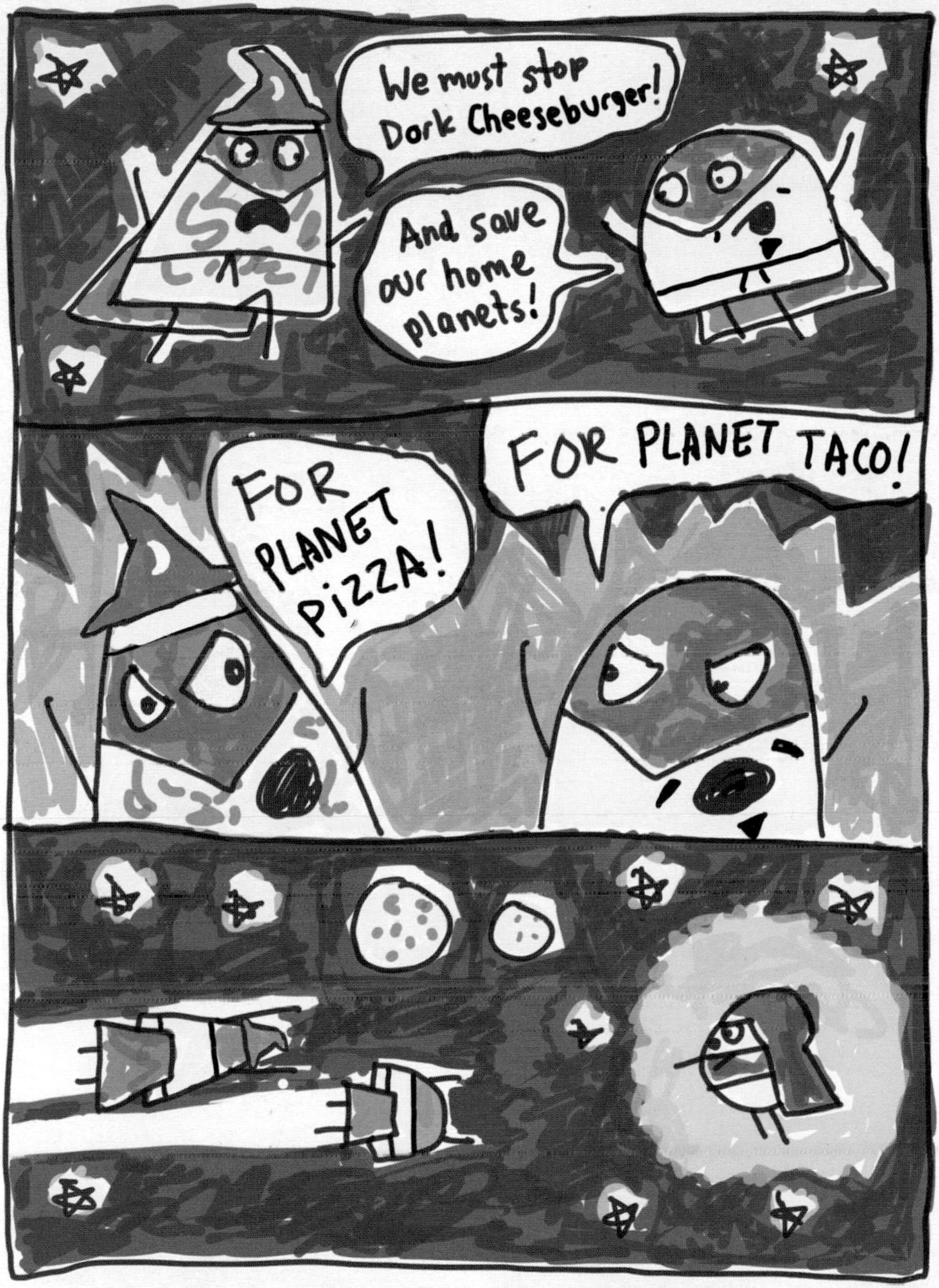
We must stop Dork Cheeseburger!
And save our home planets!
FOR PLANET PIZZA!
FOR PLANET TACO!

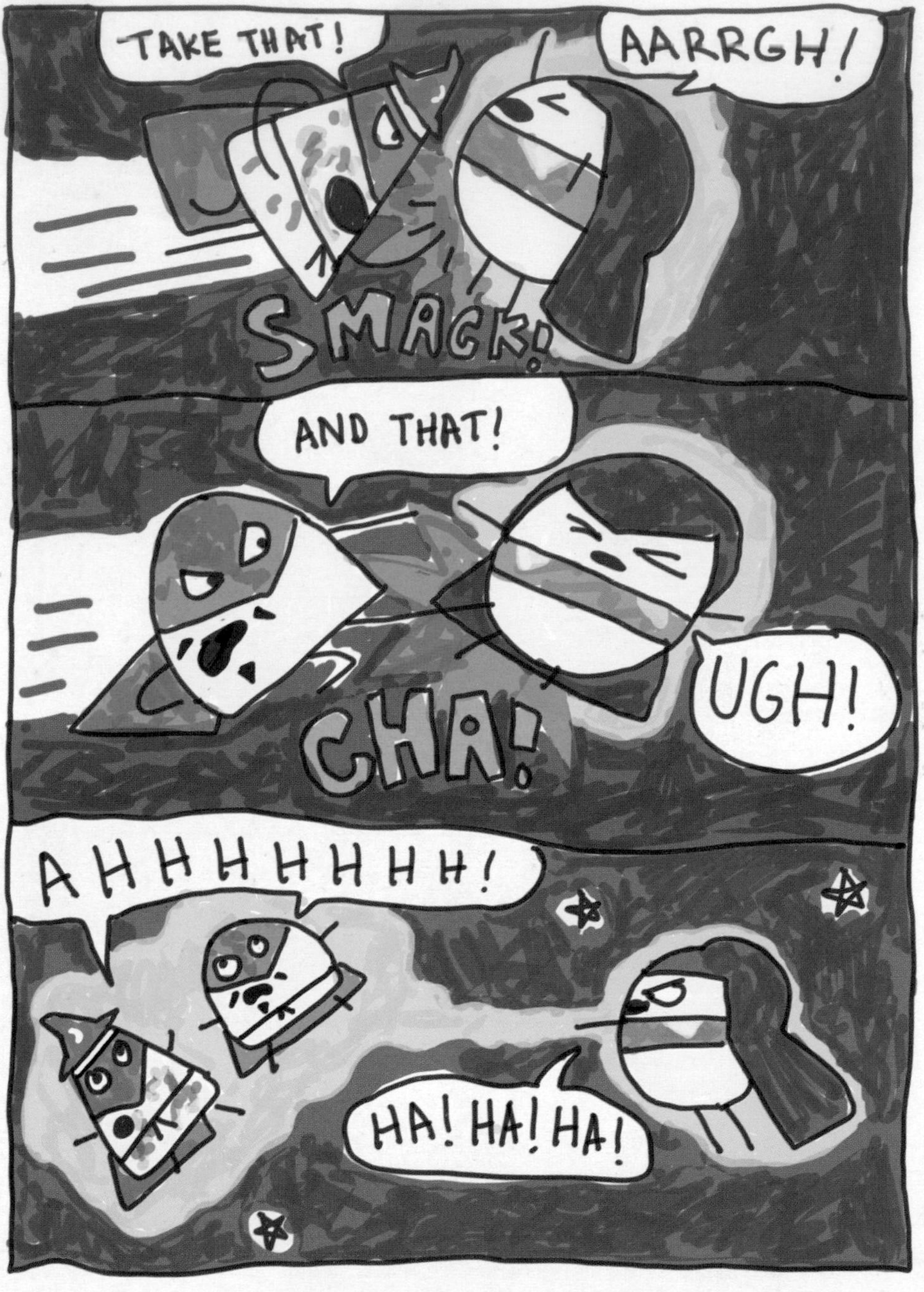
TAKE THAT!
AARRGH!
SMACK!
AND THAT!
CHA!
UGH!
AHHHHHHH!
HA! HA! HA!

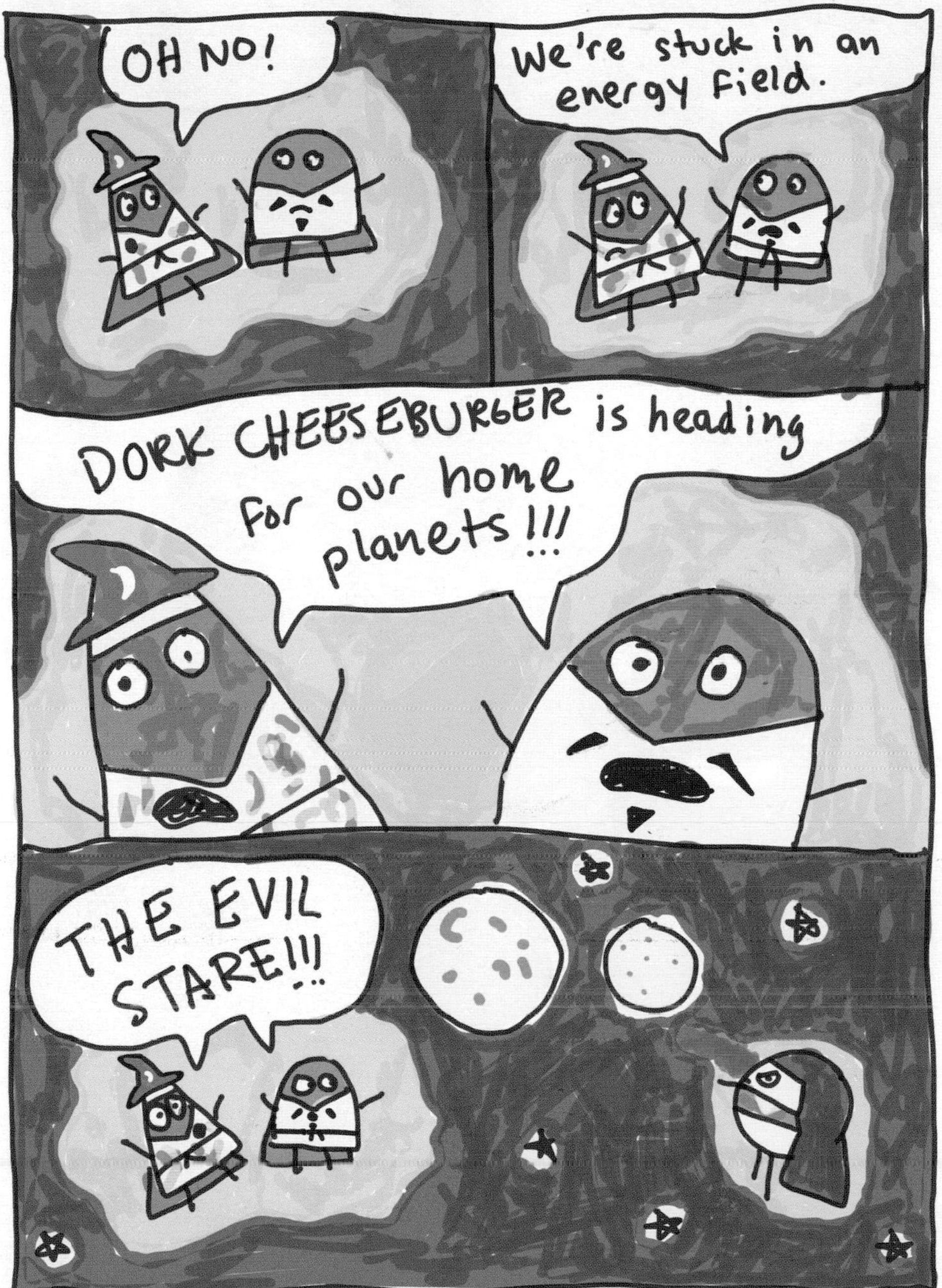
OH NO!
We're stuck in an energy field.
DORK CHEESEBURGER is heading for our home planets!!!
THE EVIL STARE!!!

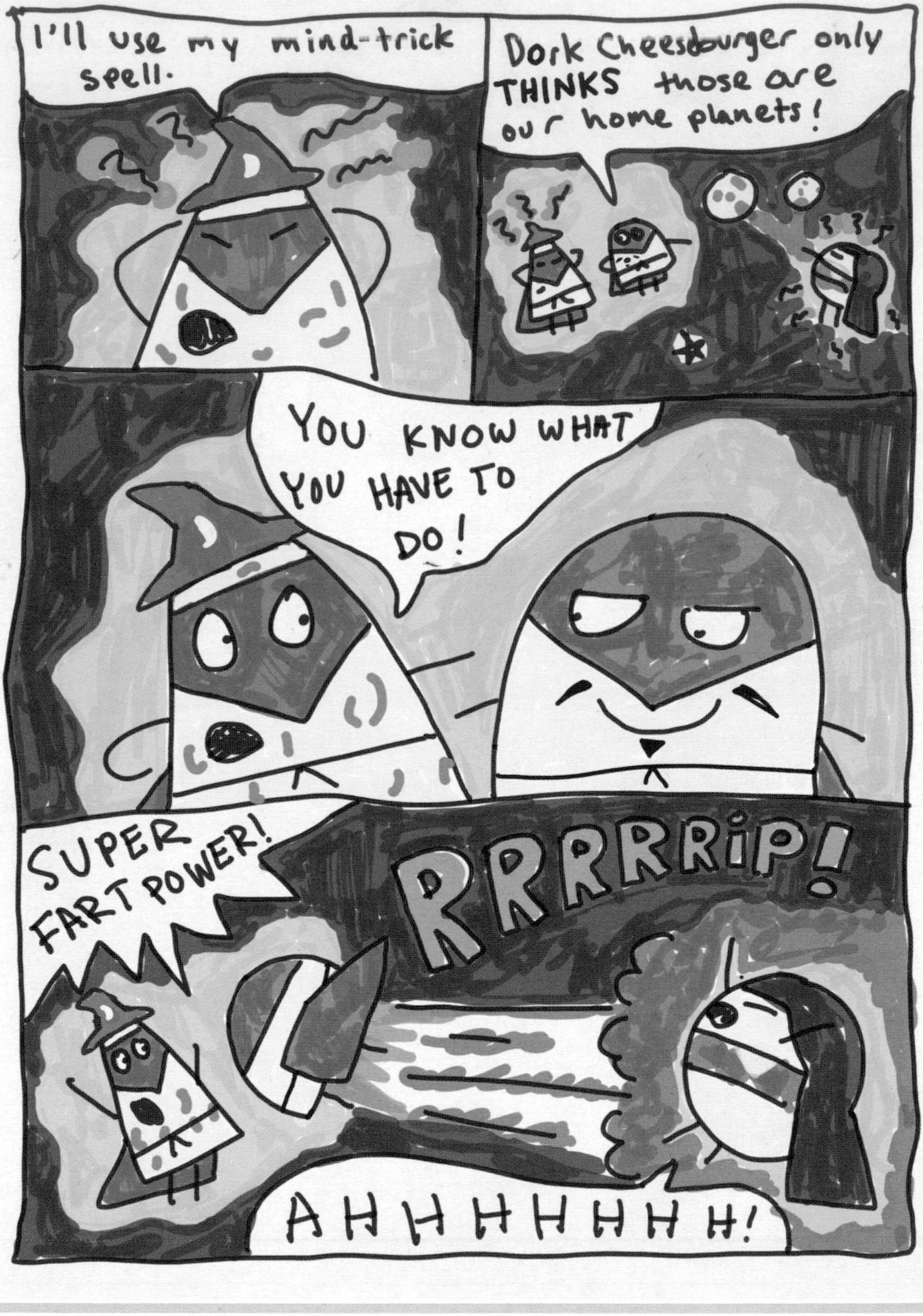
I'll use my mind-trick spell.
Dork Cheeseburger only THINKS those are our home planets!
YOU KNOW WHAT YOU HAVE TO DO!
SUPER FART POWER!
RRRRRIP!
AHHHHHHH!

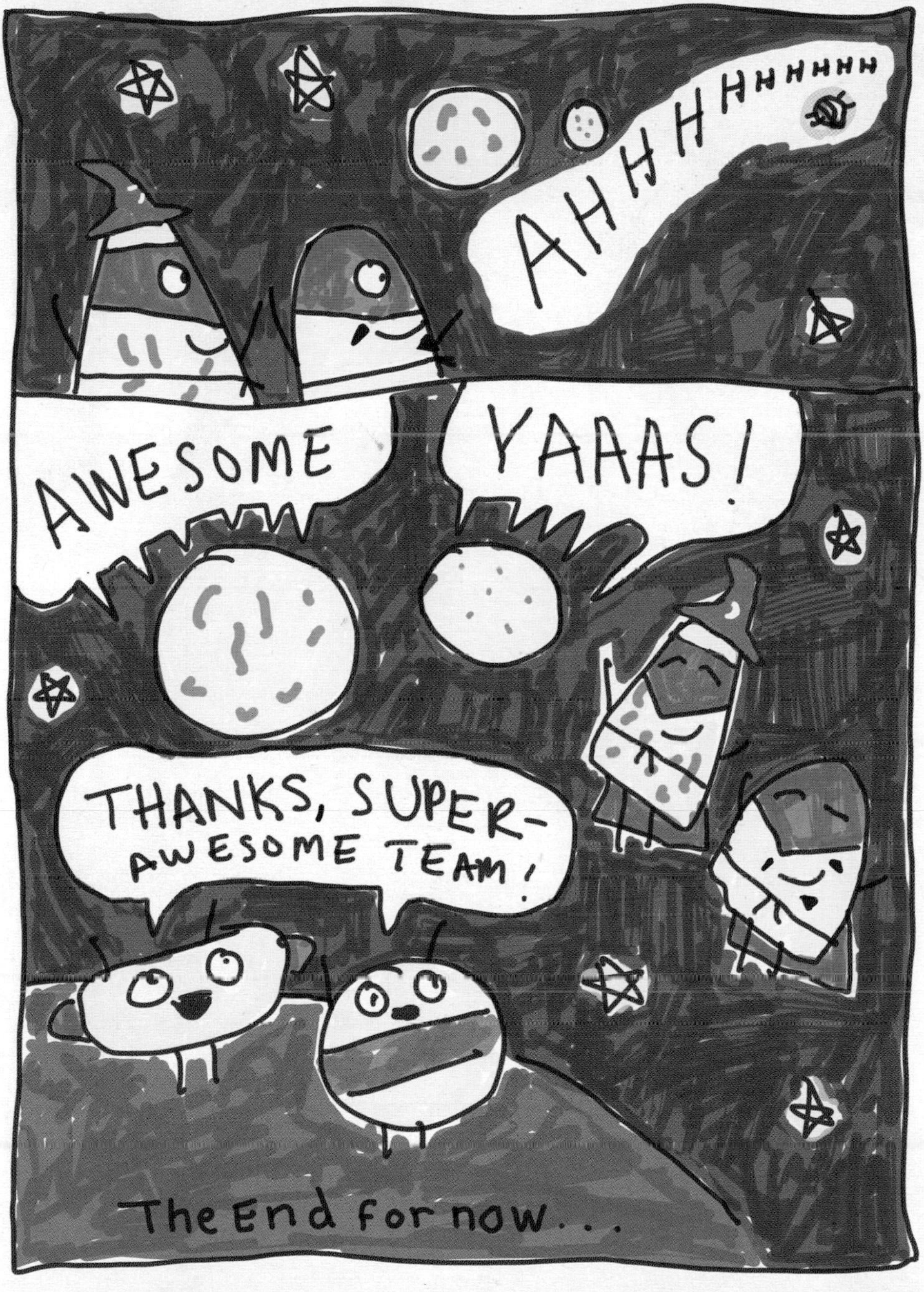
AHHHHHHHHHHH
AWESOME
YAAAS!
THANKS, SUPER-AWESOME TEAM!
The End for now...

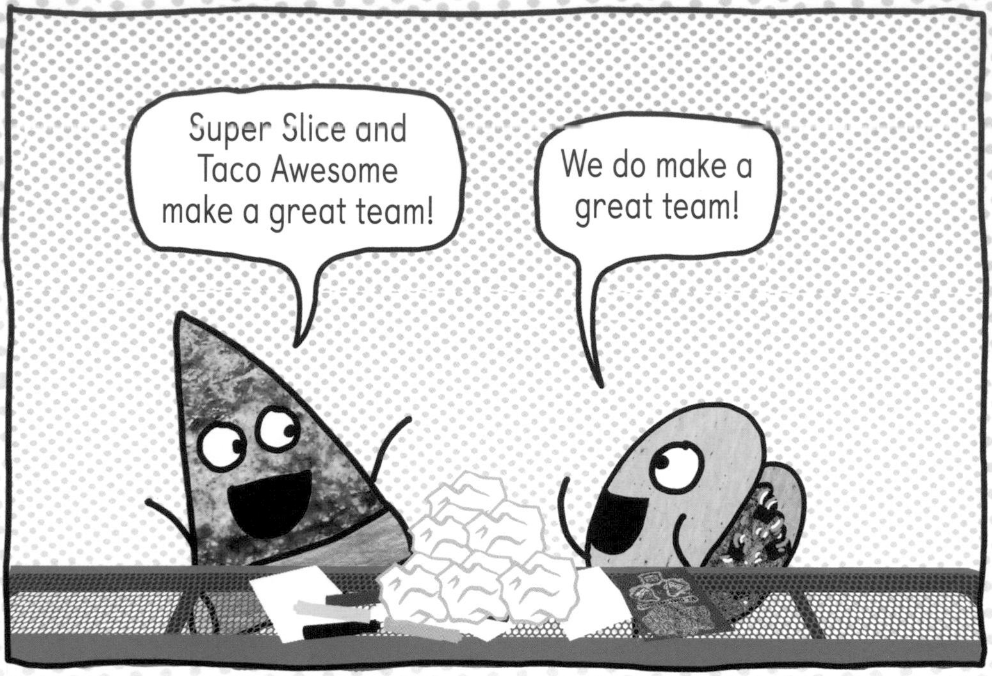
Super Slice and Taco Awesome make a great team!
We do make a great team!

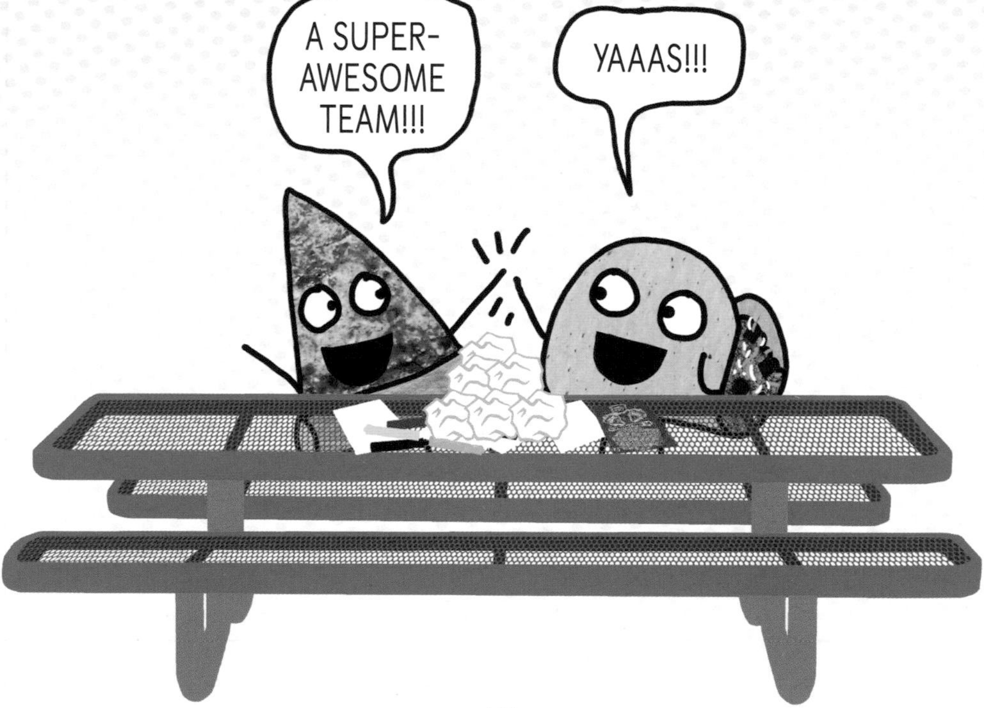
A SUPER-AWESOME TEAM!!!
YAAAS!!!

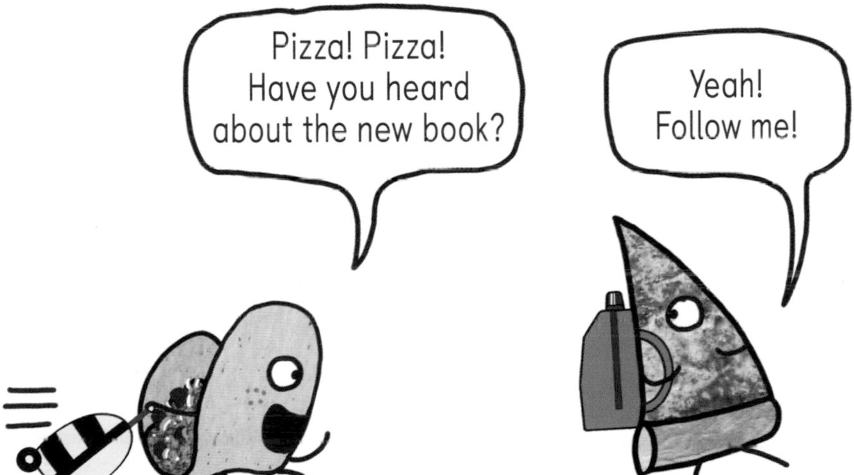
Pizza! Pizza! Have you heard about the new book?
Yeah! Follow me!

How to Be Cool

3 EASY STEPS!

1. Wear sunglasses.
2. Say "cool" and "whatever" a lot.
3. Read the next Pizza and Taco book!

PIZZA AND TACO: TOO COOL FOR SCHOOL!

Coming in Summer 2022!

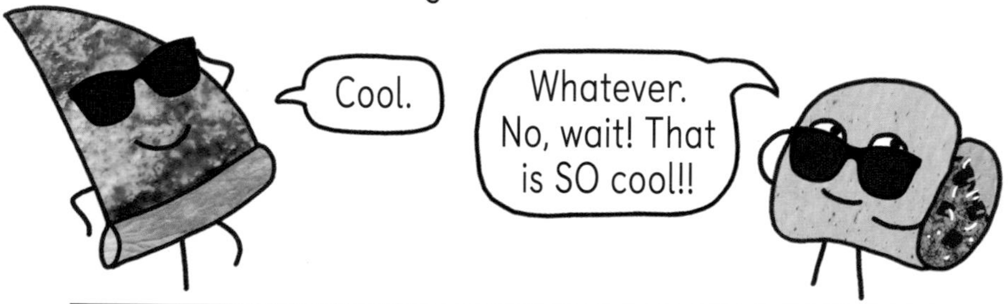
Cool.
Whatever. No, wait! That is SO cool!!

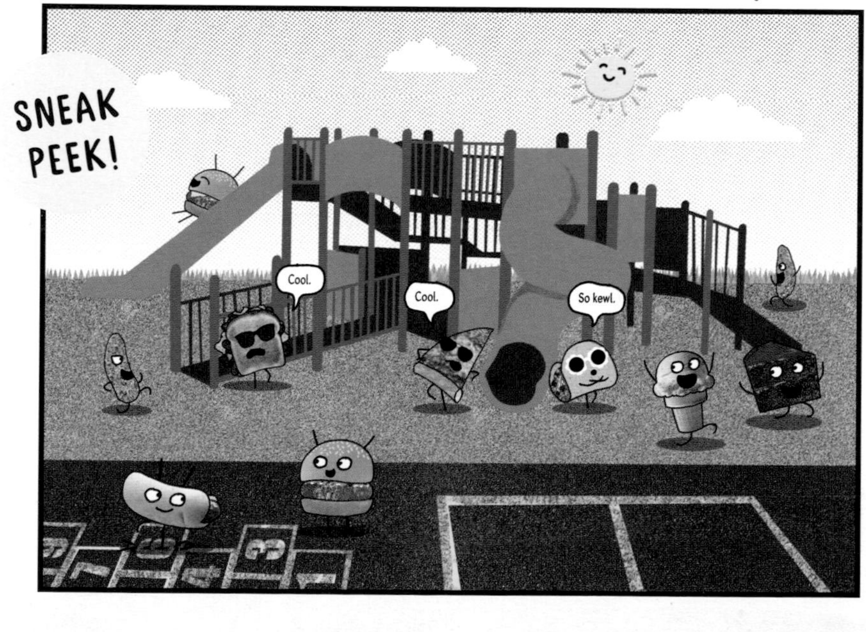
SNEAK PEEK!
Cool.
Cool.
So kewl.

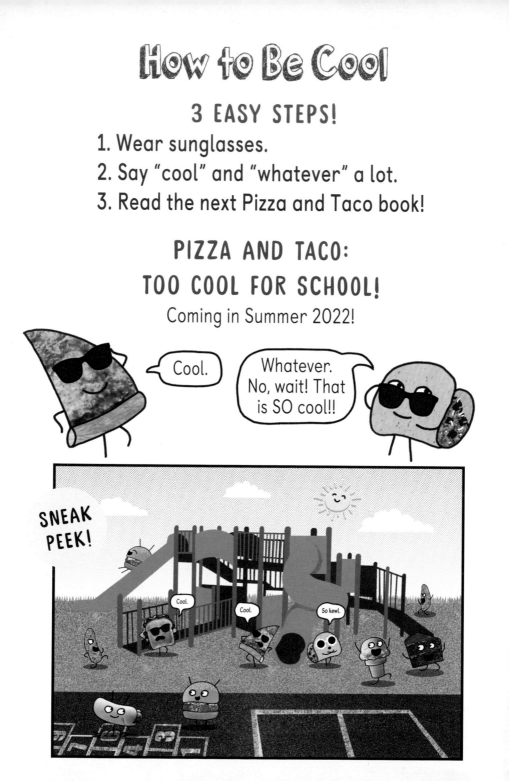

AWESOME COMICS FOR AWESOME KIDS

DONUT FEED THE SQUIRRELS

What will these squirrels do for the chance to eat the perfect donut?

SHARK AND BOT

Will this mismatched pair become best friends forever?

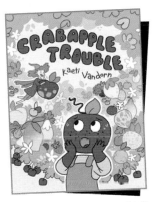

PIZZA AND TACO

Who's the best?
Find out with food, friends, and waterslides.

CRABAPPLE TROUBLE

Join Calla and Thistle as they face their fears in this magical adventure!

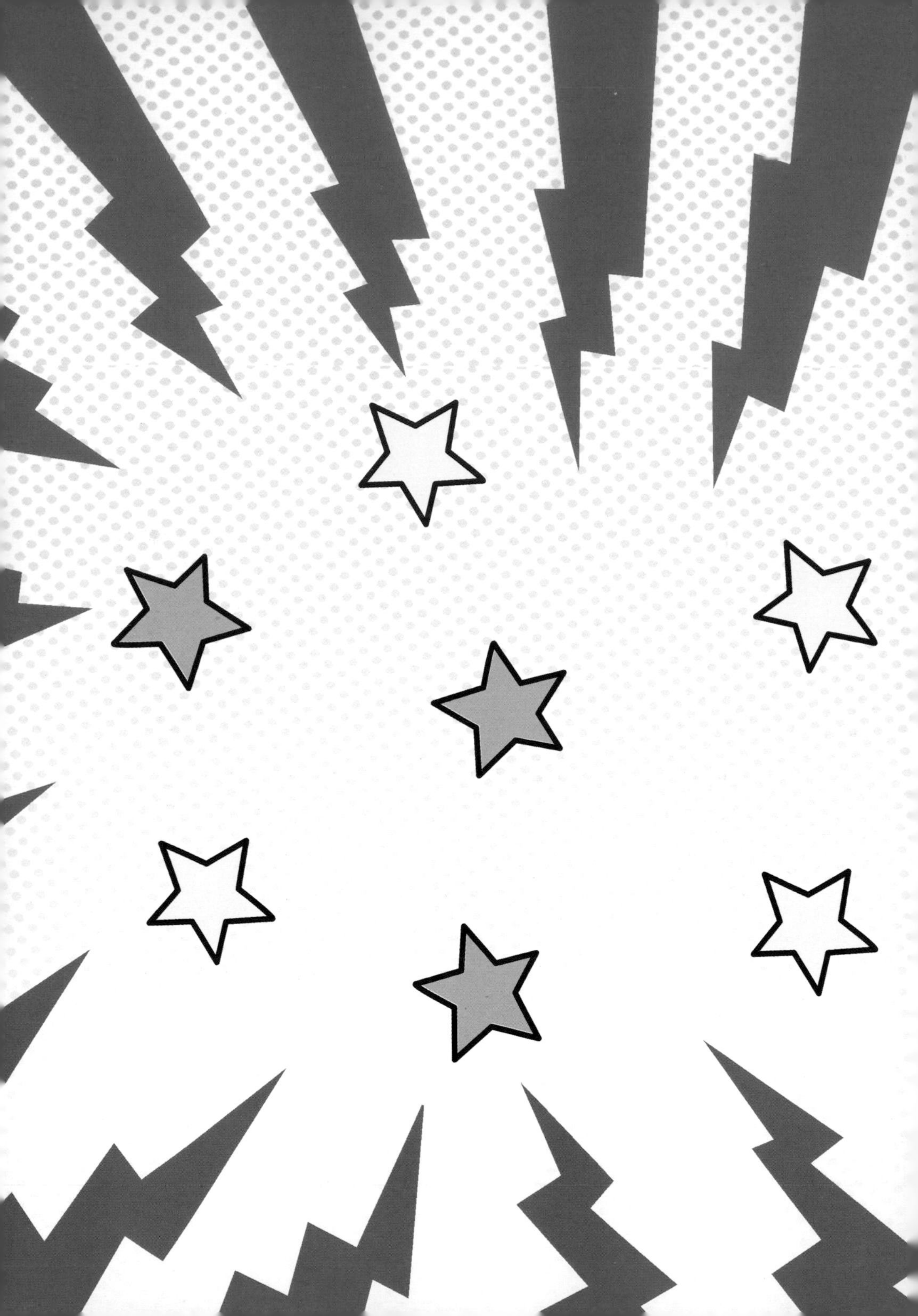